I0671430

Thief in Paris

Ivy Marie

Ivy Marie Publishing

Contents

Chapter One

Darcie

The Museum of Terra hosts many natural exhibits, such as fossils, minerals, and insects. Holst Security has been hired to protect a significant exhibition tonight and for the coming week. I arrived half an hour before the museum's closure to convene with the client. I am to put him at ease so that everything will go smoothly. The boss has found that clients are most anxious on the first day of the contract. So I also ensure there is no extra clause that the client wishes to add to the already signed agreement — a contract he would have signed with the boss.

The woman at the museum's help desk was expecting me and immediately directed me to the curator's office. With her brief directions, I approached a closed door tucked away from visitor view. I rapped my knuckles on the door twice, waiting for it to open. A man with round glasses peered out. *Not our client.*

"Darcie Manners of Holst Security." I announced.

With a curt nod, the man opened the door wider and gestured for me to enter. I assumed he was the curator. There were two other men present in the room. One of the men I recognized as our client, thanks to the picture provided in the file on this job, but I didn't recognize the other man. I eyed the one I didn't recognize. He leaned against the desk, his feet crossed at the ankles, his arms crossed over his chest. He was watching our client pace the crowded room with a hint of a smile playing on his lips.

"Mr. Bridington, my name is Darcie Manners from Holst Security." I extended my hand to the pacing man. "I am the lead on tonight's team."

"Thank you, Miss Manners." He stopped pacing to clasp my hand in his. "I've gone over the security plan your boss sent over, and I wish to make one minor adjustment."

Absolutely not! I held back my displeasure at a last-minute change. When clients choose to make a last-minute change, something always seems to go wrong.

"What might that be?" I maintained a professional tone.

He turned to the third man in the room, the one leaning on the desk. The man reached for a box on the desk next to him. Opening it, he revealed The Eye, a green emerald shaped like a cat's eye with a single dark green streak through it to emphasize its name. *Tonight's protection.* It truly is a beautiful gemstone. It was set into a necklace for the late Mrs. Bridington and is now displayed for the world.

"You see." Mr. Bridington began. "This necklace was made to be worn. As an extra security layer, I wish you to wear it."

"Excuse me?" I pulled my eyes from the gem to stare at the client dumbfounded. "That wasn't part of the contract you signed with Holst Security."

"I know." He held up his hands as if it'll placate me. "This is the first time The Eye has come out of the vault since my wife's passing. She wanted the world to admire this gemstone as much as she did. I fear thieves might come to try and steal it now that it is available."

I could hear the boss' words in my head about making the client happy while still doing the job right. *This is a bad idea.* I drew in my bottom lip, mentally reviewing my options to determine which was best in this situation. The best option would be to uphold the contract and not accept this last-minute change.

"Mr. Bridington, putting The Eye around my neck will not make it safer." I tried to reason with him.

"But it would make it harder for a thief to steal?" He countered.

"Potentially, but —"

"Please Miss Manners." He begged, taking both of my hands in his. "It would make me feel much more at ease. If it helps you decide, I have had a fake made that can be placed in the case. If a thief arrives, he'll steal that instead of the real thing."

I pulled my hands back with a sigh. "Do you intend to have me wear The Eye every night while it is in this museum?"

"It would be appreciated."

Taking a pen and paper from the curator's desk, I created an amendment to his contract, having Mr. Bridington sign it. It stated that this was his request, that Holst Security was against it and that we were not liable if something happened. I sent a picture to the boss and then folded the original into my back pocket with the phone. The unknown man placed The Eye around my neck.

Mr. Bridington teared up. "I never thought I'd see The Eye around someone's neck ever again. Thank you Miss Manners."

I tucked The Eye under my blouse, brushing my hair over my shoulders to hide any evidence of the chain. *I really don't like this.* The three men followed me to the lobby, where the team for tonight's protection was waiting. Tristan Prince — my partner — had already gone over the plan one last time with them and made sure their radios were turned to the correct channel. I took the radio he handed me. Then, instructing the others on the team to get to their posts signalled the start of tonight's job.

"Okay." I turned to the curator. "Take us to the exhibit."

The curator turned and led the way through the museum. The Eye was to be on the third floor of the museum. The third unknown man made a show of placing a fake version of The Eye into a glass case. He had scrutinized it, declaring it was real before it was locked up. Now it was up to Tristan and myself to stand guard in the silent exhibit room.

Around midnight, the air conditioner turned off, followed shortly by the lights. I called out for an update over the radio. Silent. *Something's not right.*

"Emergency lights should have turned on by now." Tristan stated.

"I agree, but we should maintain our post."

"I'll be quick as a bunny." He grinned. "Floor plans showed emergency stairs for security are nearby. Should be a breeze to get down to the basement, check out the breaker panel, then return."

"Then you stay here, and I'll go." The thought of staying here, alone, was unnerving.

"I'm faster." He stated. "Fifteen minutes, twenty tops."

"Make it quick, Tristan." My eyes darted around the shadows of the room. "I have a bad feeling."

"Gut feeling?"

I nodded. Tristan's green gaze studied me.

"I'll be extra quick, Darcie."

Would a thief be stupid enough to try and steal The Eye on the first night? Or am I just being paranoid? Tristan left me in the dark, the only light coming from the base of various displays because they are on a circuit separate from the main building. Being the only one in the room, I could hear every little sound — like a lock sliding into place on the door.

"Tristan?" I called. *Stupid, he only just left.* I pulled out my phone to use the flashlight feature and swung it around the room, trying to find the source of the soft footsteps I heard while staying close to the fake eye. "Show yourself."

"What do I have here?" A deep velvety voice purred.

A man stepped into the light of my flashlight. I couldn't see his face. I lowered the light to his chest. I still couldn't get a good enough view of him. He continued to step closer until he was only a couple of feet away. I could see his blue eyes staring at me through a black mask that covered half his face.

"A female security guard? No." He shook his head. "You don't look like museum security."

"You're pretty bold for a mere thief." I countered, standing my ground.

"Mere thief?" He chuckled. "Allow me to introduce myself." He then bent at the waist, bowing while maintaining eye contact. "I am Le Corbeau, jewel thief extraordinaire."

"Never heard of you." Then, keeping the light trained on him, I reached for the handcuffs I kept in my back pocket while on duty. "But thank you for identifying yourself, thief — now I can arrest you."

"Arrest me?" He laughed, the sound rich and decadent. "I haven't stolen anything."

"But you did break into the museum. Local police can still charge you for that."

Keeping his distance, the thief walked to the other side of the display case I'd held at my back. I could see his face more clearly with the light from the display case. He didn't wear just any mask, but one that looked very bird-like. Possibly a crow. His stunning blue eyes watched me with every step he took. Those eyes are going to haunt my dreams, especially when his lips quirked into a teasing smile. *Focus Darcie!*

"You are not going to steal The Eye."

He looked down at the display. "I wouldn't want a fake anyway."

"Fake?" I choked out. *How does he know that?*

"The Eye has a dark streak through it that moves when you do." He looked up at me. "A simple trick of the light, but it's a unique feature of its cut."

Interesting. I looked down at the fake. It certainly looks real. *How common is that little fact?* Le Corbeau took that moment to step closer to me. Lights came back on. Closing my eyes to the sudden brightness was a rookie mistake. I felt the thief's hand brush my neck. *Shit.* Training kicked in. I grabbed his wrist and swept my foot at his ankles. He fell to the ground. The momentum took me with him. His wrist still in my grip, I twisted his arm back and placed my knee into his back to keep him face down.

"You will not be taking The Eye." I told him firmly.

This thief had the gall to laugh. Then, with his free hand, he pushed himself up, knocking me off. I fell onto my back. I was not about to let him escape. Le Corbeau was halfway standing when I tackled him back to the ground. Straddling his chest, I held his wrists above his head, handcuffs still in my back pocket. I reached for them again.

"As much as I appreciate a beautiful woman straddling me." He used his body to flip our position. "I prefer you this way."

I glared up at the grinning blue-eyed thief. With my hands pinned above my head, he unbuttoned my blouse just enough to get a good look at The Eye. *Double shit!* I squirmed, trying to flip us back, but the man outweighed me. My brain raced through every training exercise to find the one that would best help my current situation. His fingers traced the chain to the back of my neck. I wiggled one leg up, placing my foot on his chest and pushed him back with all my strength. I successfully pushed him far enough back that he was forced to let go of my wrists. I turned on my stomach and crawled away before scrambling to my feet. For the third time this night, I reached for the cuffs.

"Looking for these?" He teased, my cuffs dangling from his fingers.

How? I felt for my back pocket. The cuffs I'd brought were no longer there. I glared at the silver bracelets he dangled.

"You can use those to cuff yourself." I retorted.

He laughed, far too amused. Banging at the door told me Tristan was back. Relief flooded my system. This man hadn't used any weapons but was still dangerous, and I needed help. Pulling the gun I kept at my side — only used for extreme situations — the thief's smile faded, and he slowly put up his hands.

"Use those cuffs." I ordered.

"Gladly."

He let go of something he had in his other hand. It hit the floor; thick smoke emanated out, filling the space around us. I couldn't see a thing. The door slammed open. When Tristan called out for me, I lowered my gun, not wanting to shoot any fellow Holst Security members. I felt the weapon get taken from me then my wrists got handcuffed behind my back.

"Better luck next time, Kitten." Le Corbeau whispered in my ear, then kissed my cheek.

"Thief!" I shouted. As the smoke cleared, I could see my partner and a couple of extra men but no blue-eyed thief. "Where did he go?"

"Who?" Tristan lowered his gun, taking in my appearance. "What happened?"

"Le Corbeau, the thief who came for The Eye."

He freed my wrists. Immediately I felt around my neck.

"Shit! Search this museum. Find the thief. Don't let him get away with The Eye!"

No one moved.

"Now!" I ordered.

The men turned and ran out of the room. I snagged Tristan's radio, giving the same order. I will not let this thief waltz right out of here. He couldn't have gotten far. Tristan was staring at the fake gemstone, not understanding my order. He disliked my explanation even more. I should have told him about the adjustment at the beginning.

I texted the boss. He came to the museum in the morning to manage the client and the curator. The man is a smooth political talker. With the signed amendment of the contract that I had Mr. Bridington sign the night prior, he could talk his way out of any legal action. But, unfortunately, the boss had my hide for letting a thief get close enough to steal The Eye from around my neck.

I promised him I'd find The Eye and this thief. He gave me two weeks to find some lead, or he'll hand the problem to local authorities. Tristan offered to drive me home, but I drove to the museum last night and wasn't about to leave my car behind. Once home, I stripped out of my clothes, desperately needing a shower. A business card floated to the ground. It displayed a black crow holding onto a gem in its beak — Le Corbeau. Resisting the urge to crumple the card, I took it to my home office and pinned it to the corkboard wall.

"I will hunt you down and put you behind bars."

Chapter Two

♥

Le Corbeau

Very carefully, I placed the Ruby Dragon into the safe. Stealing this from adventurers in Asia was too easy. The moment I saw their post on social media, I immediately caught a flight out, knowing others would be going after it. Unfortunately, getting it out of Asia wasn't as easy. The Browns Twins were also after the Ruby Dragon. If they had gotten their hands on it first, they would have chopped it into as many pieces as possible and sold them to the highest bidder. Once the heat on the Ruby Dragon cools off, I'll send it to a museum where it belongs.

My eyes drifted to The Eye. It's been two weeks since I stole that piece and crossed paths with the woman with defiant hazel eyes. Those eyes are burned in my memory. *I wonder what she's doing right now.* Stealing that piece from her was the most fun I've had in years, and I wish there were some way I could see her again. I shook that thought out of my head. *It's never going to happen.* I exited the hidden room in my office. Marcus was waiting for me, lounging in the chair opposite the desk.

"Do you think we can give The Eye back?" He queried.

"I'll look into it." I agreed, sliding into my chair. "But it should be safe enough."

"How was your trip?"

"Quite the adventure. I found the adventurers easily enough. But, unfortunately, so did the Browns Twins. They were hot on my tail most of the way out of Asia."

"But you lost them?" He confirmed.

"Eventually."

"The Ruby Dragon?"

I nodded toward the bookshelf that hid the entrance to the safe. "Just locked it up."

"Good." He tossed a folder on my desk. "We have a client in Paris requesting our expertise. Josephine Dubois. She has some paintings, sculptures, and jewellery she'd like appraised. Also, we still have that issue with the Paris branch."

"Book us a flight." I told him. I opened the folder to read about the appraisal request. Josephine and her husband are long-time clients. Marcus and I personally appraise the pieces for their auction house. "We'll head to Paris tomorrow morning."

Nodding, he then checked his phone. "Excuse me. I have a meeting with Holst Security."

"Holst Security?" That piqued my interest. "Why?"

"No idea." Marcus' lips quirked. "They were the security team in charge of protecting The Eye. So it could have something to do with that."

I narrowed my eyes at him, but it didn't stop the grin from fully forming before leaving my office. He knew I'd looked into the security company in charge of protecting The Eye, hoping to learn the name of the hazel-eyed woman. No luck. The company website didn't contain any pictures of their staff. *I wonder if that woman is here.*

I logged into the security feed of the building through my computer. I do not regularly spy on my employees, but this is a particular circumstance. There is no sound, but I can certainly watch the interactions. I enlarged the feed in Marcus' office.

I recognized the hazel-eyed beauty sitting in Marcus' office. *Who is that with her?* Next to her sat a male, wearing jeans and a button-down shirt, her partner maybe. Their heads were bent together, whispering to each other. Then Marcus arrived. They pulled apart, sitting up straighter. It made me curious as to what they were discussing.

Marcus shook their hands before taking his place behind his desk. He listened to his two guests speak. I watched his face sour and his shoulders straighten. It made me wish for sound. He clearly did not like what they were saying. They weren't there for long, five or maybe ten minutes. Then, finally, my mystery woman handed him a business card, which he accepted, then ushered them out.

"What was that all about?" I questioned when Marcus returned shortly to my office.

"They wanted a list of our employees and our travel itinerary."

I frowned. "Why?"

"They were tasked with tracking down The Eye and wanted to ensure no one in Rarity Inc. was involved in the theft." He scowled. "Claimed it was just a precautionary measure."

How curious. "And what did you tell them?"

"I'll have to discuss it with the CEO, and they should be prepared to be denied."

Not having turned the camera off, movement in Marcus' office caught my eye. "What do we have here?"

Marcus came around the desk to watch the woman slip back into the office and go straight to the computer. She plugged something into the system and, within a few clicks, gained access to the password-protected computer. We stared dumbfounded as we watched her open and close files. She looked up at the door as if expecting Marcus to walk through those doors any second. She pulled out what could only be assumed to be USB from the computer and left.

Marcus pointed at the screen. "She stole from us."

"Yes, she did." I'm not sure if I should be impressed or furious.

"I'm going to catch her before she leaves the building."

"Wait." I held up a hand, a smile playing on my lips. "Let her go."

"Killian."

"If you can get me her address, I'll break in and steal the information back."

Marcus shook his head. "By then, she'd have already looked at the information she stole."

"Maybe."

"And there's no guarantee she'll take the information home."

"Only one way to find out."

"Fine." He ran a hand through his hair. "She gave me her business card. So it shouldn't be too difficult to find her address."

"Thank you."

Marcus nodded and then left my office. I leaned back in my chair. I couldn't wait for tonight.

I found myself at the door of this hazel-eyed woman. It was late, and all the neighbours were sound asleep, so no one would catch me attempting to break in. I'm not skilled at lock picking, so it took a few tries, and I was extra careful not to leave any scratch marks on the lock. The woman's car wasn't in the driveway, so I figured she was still at work. At least, I hoped she was. Getting caught is not in the plans for tonight.

Once inside, I locked the door. *I'm surprised there's no alarm.* I scoured the first floor of her condo, searching for a laptop. No laptop, but I did find pictures of her with what appeared to be her parents. Her smile lit her face. I moved to the second floor. I found her bedroom, and it took everything in me not to snoop beyond the threshold. Forcing myself to step back, I entered the other room on the upper floor. A spare bedroom turned office. *Intriguing.*

I shone my phone light around, finding a wall filled with all my past and potential future heists. The Ruby Dragon was included in those possibilities. *Impressive.* I didn't have time to double-check her work. I opened the laptop that I found on the desk, surprised there was no password. I plugged in the USB I brought with me. It contains a mirror program linked to my laptop, I'll be able to see everything she does on the device, and while I'm here, I'll remove all the documents she would have taken from my company.

The upload was only at fifty percent when headlights flashed in the window. *Fuck!* I listened to the sound of keys turning in the front door lock. *She's home.* I sat at the laptop as long as I dared. Then, I heard her footsteps coming up the stairs. I closed the lid just enough so the screen's glow didn't give me away and hid in the closet. I held my breath, expecting her to enter the office. She didn't. Instead, I heard the water running and suspected she was showering.

With her in the shower, I can take a little more time to get this mirroring program up and running. I returned to the laptop as quietly as possible to see its progress — seventy percent. The water stopped running. I dimmed the screen as much as possible and lowered the lid again. I heard a drawer open and close, then another. If I moved from the chair now, she could potentially hear me. With the hope that she went to bed, I re-opened the laptop and brightened the screen enough for me to see the progress. Lights flared on above me.

"Turn around, slowly." Came the order. Her eyes widened as I obeyed. "Le Corbeau."

"Hello Kitten." I graced her with a charming smile, ensuring I blocked her view of the laptop.

She narrowed her eyes, hands tightening on the grip of her gun. A set of handcuffs dangling from one hand. "What are you doing here?"

I perused her body leisurely. *What a vision.* She wore shorts and a tank top, accentuating a shapely body. My cock hardened at the sight of her. After our tussle at the museum, I already know what it feels like to have her under me. Now I wonder what it'll feel like to touch all those curves. The tank top couldn't hide the hard nipples that poked at the fabric. As my eyes came up to her face, I could see a hint of pink on her cheeks. She knew her body was reacting to my perusal, but she didn't want to announce it by trying to hide the evidence.

"What are you doing here?" She repeated.

"Enjoying the view." I answered her question.

She scowled in response. "Why are you here? In my home? Which, by the way — how do you know where I live?"

"So many questions." Very slowly, I lowered my hands, placing them on the chair arms. "Curious, are we, Kitten?"

"I'm curious as to what you look like in orange."

"Orange isn't my colour. However, black is much more slimming. Wouldn't you agree it's more my colour?"

She tossed the handcuffs at my feet. "Put those on."

"Are we going to do this again?"

"You're trespassing on private property, thief."

I looked down at the silver cuffs. "If you want me in them so badly, you'll have to do it yourself."

The gun lowered a fraction, but she didn't move closer. "I'm not going anywhere near you."

"Now, that is unfortunate."

I could see the debate going on in her mind. She hasn't called the cops yet, which could be a good sign. *I wonder, how far can I tease her?* The gun fell to her side, and she cocked a hip, her eyes perusing me. Her gaze was filled with both interest and suspicion. It heated my skin, arousing me further.

"See something you like, Kitten?"

"Why do you call me that?" She frowned.

"Clearly, it is because I don't know your name."

"And if you knew my name, would you still call me that?"

I shrugged. "I think it fits you. Cute but has claws."

The already subtle blush in her cheeks deepened. "Did my trip to Rarity Inc. scare you?"

Talk about a change of subject. I gestured to the wall she's made of me. "Did you miss me?"

"I want you in handcuffs."

"Handcuffed to the bed?" I grinned. "All you have to do is ask."

That caused the blush to deepen further and her eyes to dilate. *This is getting fun.* She put the gun on the floor to cross her arms. The movement drew my eyes to the lush mounds she pushed up. They nearly spilled out of the tank top. My mouth salivated, and my hands tightened on the armchair. I wanted to touch those breasts of hers. I wanted to have them in my mouth.

I licked my lips. "I would gladly let you have your way with me."

"Why are you using an appraisal company? Can you not find your spoils without them?"

"I can steal whatever I put my mind to." I flashed her a seductive smile.

"Mmm." She hummed, finally moving forward.

Her hips swayed deliberately. My cock pulsed against the zipper of my pants. She bent forward at the waist, picking up the handcuffs, providing me with an unobstructed view down her shirt.

"So, you decided to put your mind into breaking into my home. Were you planning to steal the information I didn't take from Rarity Inc.? Or did you miss me that much?"

"I missed you terribly, Kitten."

Wait, did not take? Did I walk into a trap? Her eyes danced with amusement as she stopped within arms reach. I wanted to pull her into my lap, run my fingers through her wet hair, and kiss her. But I need to be careful with our cat-and-mouse game.

"And what information do you think I would need to steal from you?" I questioned, voice tight.

She smiled playfully, the handcuffs swinging from her fingers. "Now, now, Corbeau, I can't just give you all the answers. But I have to ask — did you not find it suspicious that there were no obstructions for you to disarm?"

I did walk into a trap! Very carefully, I stood, keeping her view of the laptop blocked while removing the USB. "You wanted me here."

"I did."

"Yet you're not going to arrest me."

She tossed the handcuffs onto the desk. "Not yet."

"Why?" It's my turn to be suspicious.

"That, my dear thief, is for me to know and for you to find out."

She leaned into me, her soft body pressing against mine. Her fingers danced along the bottom of my mask. I sucked in a breath, unsure if I wanted her to pull it off or not. Then, with a determined look in her eyes, she pushed herself away and took a step to the side, clearing a path to the exit.

"Until next time Corbeau."

Fuck! I was so excited to see her again that I didn't think beyond that. It never occurred to me that this could be a trap. Now she knows I either work at Rarity Inc. or with someone within the company. The only saving grace is that she doesn't know I'm the company's CEO. I should have immediately realized something was wrong when no alarm was activated in her condo. She works for a security company. There's no way she wouldn't have her own security set up. *Sneaky little Kitten.*

Chapter Three

♥

Darcie

Earlier this week, the boss called in a favour with a friend at the FBI. He entertained the idea of a thief going by Le Corbeau. He became a believer when I showed him my hours of research into past thefts. The FBI has authority in Canada only if local law enforcement invites them to assist in a case, so he is helping me off the books.

The first thing I did when I went to work was track him down. I knew he'd be at the Holst Security office early like he had been all week. I found Agent Kent Moore in the break-room doctoring a coffee. I placed my laptop on the closest table and sidled up next to him to make myself a coffee. I was excited, practically vibrating, waiting to tell him about last night's visit. He smiled pleasantly, handing me the sugar. I then went to the fridge for a hazelnut cream.

He leaned against the coffee counter, watching me. "What are you dying to tell me?"

"Le Corbeau stopped by last night."

"Really?" He raised a brow. "I honestly didn't think your trap would work."

"He did something to my laptop." I took a seat at a table and tapped the device.

"I'll look into it." He joined me at the table, pulling it closer. "Have you ever considered joining the FBI?"

"Never considered it." I sipped the coffee. "I rather enjoy being at Holst Security."

"You could do great things in the Bureau. You're an amazing investigator Miss Manners, and I'd love to work with you more."

He was leaning in, flirting. Agent Moore is a good-looking man with a strong jawline, neatly trimmed beard, short brown hair, and kind brown eyes with golden flecks. He appears datable. Except I won't date another man connected to law enforcement, bad memories. However, he does seem like a nice person, trustworthy. Also, there's something about Le Corbeau's blue eyes that sets my skin on fire when he looks at me. It's a little hard to ignore that kind of reaction.

I smiled pleasantly at him. "I don't think the boss would appreciate it if you poached his staff."

Agent Moore laughed. A warm, rich sound. "Our friendship will survive."

"What's going on here?" Tristan entered the breakroom and took a seat at the table.

"Just discussing next moves." I explained. "Our trap worked. Le Corbeau stopped by for a visit, and now Agent Moore will take my laptop to figure out what he did to it."

"What exactly is the next step?"

"First, I need to figure out what this thief did to this laptop." Agent Moore tapped the device. "Then we can figure out our exact next steps. As promised, I've kept this case out of the bureau's hands, but someone is bound to catch on. Especially since I'll need to call a friend in the bureau, a tech expert, to help me dive into this laptop."

"Don't dive too deep." I warned.

"Your secrets will be safe with me, Miss Manners." Agent Moore flashed a grin.

"What will happen if the FBI gets a hold of this case?" Tristan questioned.

"They will take over." Agent Moore answered honestly. "The two of you will be forced to step aside."

I chewed my bottom lip, not liking his answer. If the FBI takes over the case, I may never see Le Corbeau in handcuffs. An image of him handcuffed to my bed flashed in my mind. *Stupid thief.* He put that tantalizing image there. My body's reaction to him last night was... overwhelming. I had seen the desire in his gaze and hoped it would be in my favour to seduce answers from him. It didn't work. Instead, I had to go for another shower after he left — a cold one.

My ringing phone interrupted my thoughts and our conversation.

"Darcie Manners."

"Bonjour." An unknown female voice answered. Her voice sounded raw and timid. "Veronica à été arrêtée."

"Arrested? What for?" Panic gnawed at my gut.

"Meurtre."

"Murder!" I was on my feet, the chair clattering to the floor. *That can't be right.* "Is this some kind of sick joke?"

"Je suis désolée." She whispered, sounding genuinely sorry. "Veronica asked me to call."

I know it was rude to hang up, but I couldn't listen anymore. The news had my brain spinning and my blood pumping. Veronica and I have been best friends since high school — she's more cheerleader preppy than a cold-blooded killer. *I need to sit down. No, I need to get to Paris.* Numbly, I picked up the chair and slid it back against the table.

"Darcie, what's wrong?" Tristan stood.

"I have to—." My voice caught. "I have to go to Paris. I'm sorry, Agent Moore."

"Go, Miss Manners, it sounds important." Agent Moore urged. He also stood and collected my laptop. "I'll keep you updated, and if you need anything, just call me."

I rushed out of the breakroom heading straight to the boss' office. I barged in. I was not giving him a chance to berate me for my rudeness and demanded time off. He raised a questioning brow. I provided him with a brief reason for my sudden need for time off. He calmly reminded me of Le Corbeau. This is far more important, I told him. I suspected he wanted to double-check where my priorities were. With a simple nod, the boss gave me his approval. He also reminded me that Holst Security has no authority or friends in the Paris police department.

Don't worry, Vee. I'm coming. I raced home to pack and buy a ticket for the soonest flight out. I don't know how long I'll be in Paris or know my action plan when I land, but at least I'll have a long flight to figure it all out. But, of course, the main priority when I land is to get her out of jail and off the suspect list.

I was lucky enough to catch an early afternoon flight. Once in my seat, I mentally calculate how long until I can be at Veronica's side. A ten-hour flight, plus Paris is six hours ahead, meant I wouldn't land until early morning the next day. *Too long*. I tried to get a little shut-eye but couldn't get my mind to settle. Between Veronica and Le Corbeau, I couldn't shut my brain off.

Landing in Paris, I redialed the number from the woman who called me about Veronica. I need to know which police station she's being held at. *Voicemail*. I'll try again in a little while. In the meantime, I rented a car and tracked down a hotel near the airport. Again, I tried calling the number. Again, I reached voicemail.

Waiting and not knowing is killing me. So instead of staying useless in the hotel room, I went out to find a coffee place. I need that phone call to tell me where Veronica is being held. I ordered a coffee and croissant, then returned to the rental car. Just over an hour after landing, I finally got that phone call I'd been waiting for.

"Darcie Manners."

"Vous avez essayé de m'appeler?" The woman questioned me.

"Yes. I'm in Paris, and I want to see Veronica."

"Where are you?" She spoke in accented English for my benefit.

"Good question." I looked out the windshield. "I can confirm that I am sitting in the car I rented outside a café I found."

She let out a soft pillowy sweet laugh. "I'll send you an address."

She hung up, and in a few moments, I received the text. I entered the address into the GPS. It had me weaving through the unknown city. Eventually, I ended up at a police station. A simple building that blended seamlessly with the surrounding buildings. I found a visitor spot and entered the police station. There was a tall brunette standing by a welcome desk. Not just tall, she was thin and beautiful, and her clothes formed perfectly to her body. I couldn't picture that woman being a cop. When I entered the building, she immediately strode my way.

"Darcie Manners?" She questioned.

My name sounded so pretty with her accent. "Yes."

She handed me a visitor's pass. "My name is Detective Marie Decesar. I'll take you to see Veronica — but you won't have much time."

Why not? "Are you the one who called me?"

"Shh." She looked around to ensure no one was around. "I am."

Suspicious. The detective led me past the front desk and down some stairs. This new area was darker, with windowless cement walls and barred doors. *The holding cells.* Partway down the third row, my best friend lay on a thin mattress. The blond-haired, blue-eyed woman looked at me, rubbed her eyes then blinked. Tears filled her eyes, and she flung herself at the bars. I reached through to wipe at the tears on her cheeks.

"I'm here, Vee." I haven't seen her this dishevelled since her high school breakup.

"Paul is dead." She sobbed.

Paul is dead? How? I took in a sharp breath at the announcement. I need to stay calm for her.

"Tell me what happened."

With guidance, I helped her remember the beginning of the day up to when she found Paul's body and was arrested. I listened carefully, trying to find something I could use to convince the local police that she was innocent. *But wait!* I perked up at the end of her story. *Right there.*

"When did you call the police?"

"What?" Veronica sniffled, trying to collect herself after rehashing the horrible ordeal.

"When did you call the police?" I repeated. "You said you found Paul, and then the police arrived to arrest you."

"I— I—." She stammered as she tried to find the answer. "I didn't."

I turned to Marie. This should be enough to be at least suspicious enough not to be holding the wife as a suspect. Unfortunately, I didn't get a chance to point this out. An officer and a decently dressed man came down the row. He glared at Marie and began scolding her. The officer pushed me aside to collect Veronica. I told her not to say a word and turned back to Marie, who was still being scolded.

"Veronica is innocent." I stated after it became just the two of us.

"Je sais." She exhaled a tired sigh. "This is Detective Giome's case."

"Was that him?"

"Oui."

"Can you not aide Veronica?" I snipped.

"C'est aussi mon amie!" Marie snapped at me. "I am not allowed near this case."

"What can you do to help her?" I retorted harshly. "I can't do anything. I am not a cop, I have no authority in Paris, but you do."

The woman stared at me. *Is she going to cry?*

"I don't want to see Veronica behind bars any more than you do." Marie guided me back up the stairs.

Just as I stepped outside, my phone began to ring. "Darcie Manners."

"Miss Manners, I have news."

"Agent Moore?" The call was jarring in my present situation.

"Are you okay? You sound distant."

"Well, I am in Paris."

There was a soft chuckle before he explained his reason for calling. "I got into your laptop."

"That was faster than I expected."

"Le Corbeau placed a mirroring program on the device."

I frowned. "Now, why would a thief do that?"

"No idea, but there's more."

I could practically hear the smile in his voice.

"He's in Paris."

I stopped in my tracks. "How? When?"

"FBI has a database that can flag clue words that any police station enters into their systems. So I entered a few keywords for Le Corbeau, hoping it might help with the case."

"What are you getting at Agent Moore?"

"Paris put Le Corbeau's calling card into their system, associated with a murder."

By now, I've reached the rental car but haven't gotten in yet. "That can't be our thief. Le Corbeau has never murdered anyone, at least not what I could find in my research."

"I agree. Based on when they entered it into their system Le Corbeau was visiting you."

I knew it. "Does this mean you're coming to Paris?"

"Why would I do that?" He questioned playfully. "I have a colleague already there."

"Who?"

"That would be you, Miss Manners."

"Agent Moore, I can't, not right now."

"The murder victim is Paul Laplume." He rushed to say.

I nearly dropped my phone. "Say that again?"

"Paul Laplume is the murder victim. The timing lines up with your sudden departure to Paris."

"Agent Moore."

"Yes Miss Manners?"

"I could kiss you."

He laughed. "I look forward to that when you return, Darcie."

"Kent." I gasped his name, shocked.

I was only teasing, but it didn't sound like he was. Calling him by his first name, I shouldn't have done that. I need to keep things professional between us. I don't want a relationship with another law enforcement personnel.

"The captain is aware of your arrival. Call me if you need anything."

I returned to the police station. This gives me a reason to stick my nose into the case. Even better, I can get Veronica free — quite possibly even today. Then, once she is out from behind those bars, I can focus on Le Corbeau.

Chapter Four

Le Corbeau

Marcus and I signed into our Paris hotel. The bellhops then took our bags up. We didn't stay. Instead, we turned and went back out the front door. It would be best to get a jump on our issue here at the Paris branch of Rarity Inc. This trip was meant as a surprise visit.

Marcus and I toured the building. The staff on the main floor were pleasant, fielding our questions with efficiency and a friendly smile. They were there to greet guests and guide them to the proper floor or expert to help them best. The next three floors were for various categories: furniture and antiques, art, and restoration. I left Marcus to tour the two floors of furniture and art while I went to the restoration. Rarity Inc. is a company for restoration and appraisals. In addition, we help out auction houses and have a small team scouring yard sales and abandoned buildings for pieces that have value that we can sell. We started to sell items roughly two years ago.

I stopped at someone carefully soldering pins to a music drum for an antique music box. The work was being done so precisely that it'll be difficult to tell that a pin or two were ever missing. The exterior had been restored with pieces of ivory, just like the original picture the client would have brought for the restorer. *Impressive.* I moved on to someone restoring a teddy bear. According to the employee, it's a sentimental piece of the client. Originally it belonged to the client's great-grandmother. She was a little girl during the Second War, and the teddy bear was given to her by her mother, a nurse, during that time. Now the client wishes to gift it to her granddaughter.

The staff were knowledgeable and courteous, revealing a passion for their work and kindness to their clients. I'm proud to have them on the Rarity Inc. team. Marcus joined me as I was bout ready to talk to the manager for this branch.

"I'm not finding any issues with the staff." He whispered.

"Me neither." I agreed. "We should head up and speak with Benoit and review the reports."

Marcus nodded. Benoit, the branch manager, was surprised to see us. The older man seemed to pale as we strolled into his office.

"Mr. Pinot, Mr. Lux, this is quite a surprise." Benoit squeaked. He cleared his throat. "What do I owe this honour?"

"We're in Paris for other business." I explained. "Decided to pop on in and see how this branch is doing."

"Operations are running smoothly."

"We've noticed. The staff we've met are experts in their fields."

"Not all of them." Benoit corrected me. "Many of them were trained by the few experts I do have."

"Impressive." I nodded.

Benoit smiled tentatively. "They have learned fast."

"I'd like to have a look at sale reports." Marcus interrupted.

"Just down the hall Mr. Lux."

Marcus left the office. Benoit appeared very nervous over Marcus' departure. I sat in one of the lush, high-back chairs in the corner of the office.

"Come sit." I gestured to the other chair. "Let's catch up. It's been a few years, Benoit."

"Of course, Mr. Pinot."

"How's your wife and children?"

Partway down into the chair, Benoit froze for a millisecond. "My wife left me three years ago and took my children with her. No, that's not accurate. They are old enough to decide and choose to go with her."

"I'm sorry." I frowned. "You two were married for what, twenty years?"

He shrugged. "We married young."

"But you still wear your ring."

"I, uh." Benoit spun the band around his finger. "I re-married."

I blinked. "Well, congratulations then."

"What about you?" He tried to shift the attention off him. "Still living the bachelor life?"

"I am."

"Ever thought of settling down?"

"Haven't met a woman who made me think to do so."

I thought about the hazel-eyed woman. I briefly considered a future with her and debated if my answer was too quickly spoken. Nevertheless, she intrigues me enough to consider a relationship.

Benoit beamed. "It does wonders on the soul to have a wife waiting for you when you come home. Her smile and love ease the stress of the day away."

Again, I thought of my hazel-eyed Kitten. *I doubt she'd be happy to be a stay home wife.* The door to the office opened, and a woman walked in. Tall, curvy, blonde, and young. She turned to Benoit and smiled, completely ignoring me. She wore a red summer dress that hit her mid-thigh, the skirt flaring out when she turned. I had caught a flash of nothing underneath. *Who is she?*

"Benoit." She cooed. "Es-tu prête pour le déjeuner?"

"Je ne peux pas. J'ai une réunion d'affaires." Benoit stood to greet her. "Giselle, this is my boss Mr. Pinot."

Her smile widened as she took me in, then extended a hand. "Enchanté."

I accepted her hand. "I am sorry to have interrupted your lunch plans."

"Vous pouvez vous joindre à nous."

"No, thank you."

Benoit wrapped an arm around her waist. "Can we reschedule those plans for supper?"

Giselle pouted. "Je suppose que oui."

I cleared my throat. "Go for lunch. I'll set up a formal meeting with your secretary for later this week."

Benoit initially looked hesitant, but Giselle's hand on his chest slid lower, and his decision was made. He thanked me for my kindness and left the office. I waited thirty seconds before following and stopping at the secretary's desk to schedule a time later this week to have a formal meeting. Upon inquiring, the secretary informed me that Giselle is Benoit's new wife. The tone of distaste told me she disapproved.

I joined Marcus in the filing room. "What do you have?"

"I think Benoit is stealing from the company." He announced.

"For how long?"

"Nearly two years."

I scowled. "That's probably how long he's been with his new wife."

"New wife?"

"She's young, at least half his age."

Marcus frowned. "Benoit is a sugar daddy?"

I grinned. "I have an appointment with Benoit later this week. This can't go on."

"What are you going to do?"

"I have no idea."

Marcus returned the files he was examining. "As a precaution, let's look at the employee files. Maybe there's someone in there who can replace Benoit. If that's the direction you choose to go."

I don't want to let Benoit go. He's been the head of the Paris branch since the beginning, and he's been very loyal to Rarity Inc. Unfortunately, Marcus has a point. If I decide to let Benoit go, I must have a replacement candidate ready. We poured over the employee files, finding three possible candidates. After making photocopies, we talked to each one casually to get a feel for their personality and their thoughts on the company.

By the time we left, I was starving. Marcus and I stopped at Café Valentin, a bistro near our hotel. The first food we'd had since landing. After our early supper, Marcus decided to return to the hotel. I stayed, sidling up to the bar for a drink or two, my decision on what I would do about Benoit forefront of my mind.

Downing the last of my first drink, three women walk into the café. I could see them through the bottom of the glass. *I must be imagining things.* Lowering the glass for a better look at the women. *That's impossible. I left her back on the other side of the globe.* I rubbed my tired eyes. Yep, that's my little Kitten. The smile she shared with the other women seemed forced. There was a tension in her body that begged the question — what caused it? She wasn't that tense when I saw her only a day ago.

I continued to watch them, to watch her. *Why is she even here?* The only way to know the answer is to ask, but I'll have to separate her from the others. The trio ordered food and a drink. They chatted and laughed and ate. I watched, waiting for the best time to steal her attention from the women she came in with.

She pushed her plate away. At that moment, I had the bartender send over a drink. *This probably won't work.* I watched the waiter take it to her, watched her eye the drink suspiciously, then look in my direction. I offered her my most charming smile while tipping my second drink in salute, hoping to lure her over.

She scowled. The other women with her glanced over. They seemed more excited that I sent her a drink than she did. I watched as they leaned in and chatted. Finally, Kitten sighed, picked up the glass and came over. I didn't realize I was holding my breath until she began to come over, and I let out a sigh of relief.

"There must have been an error." She stated, placing the drink on the bar. "Your drink was delivered to the wrong table."

"No error." I assured her. "The drink brought you to me."

She glared. "I am not interested in whatever it is you're offering."

"How about a conversation?"

My stomach tightened as I waited for her answer. A mixture of fear and excitement. Fear she'll recognize me as Le Corbeau and excitement that I can talk to her as myself. *Please don't go.* The longer she stared at me, debating her next move, the more I wanted to reach out to kiss her, to make a choice for her.

"Conversation?" She repeated skeptically. "That's it?"

"You were looking a little tense. I thought you might have wanted a change of scenery and could use a stranger to talk to."

She looked back at the women who were watching us. Something was going through that pretty mind of hers. I itched to know what it was. Then, with a sigh, she slid into the seat beside me.

"Okay, stranger, tell me about yourself."

I couldn't help but inwardly cheer at the small victory. "I don't want to brag, but I'm the CEO of a company I started from scratch."

"Yeah, no need to brag." She rolled her eyes, unimpressed.

"You asked." I put my hands up defensively. "It's not an easy job. Today was especially tough."

"What happened?"

"Unfortunately, I discovered that one of my employees has been stealing from me. Now I have to deal with it."

"Has he been with the company long?" Sympathy crept into her tone.

"Seven years and in a leadership role." I lifted my drink to my lips. "Thankfully, he's only been stealing for about two years."

"I'm sorry." She stated solemnly, reaching for the drink I sent to her earlier. "That would be heartbreaking."

"More like disappointing." I watched the amber liquid from my glass swirl as I spun it gently on the bar surface. "What about you? What do you do?"

"I'm an employee of a private security firm."

"Is it located here in Paris?"

"Canada, actually. Why?" Suspicion returned to her tone.

Is she always this suspicious? "I don't hear a French accent in your speech. Just wondering if you're local or on vacation."

"Neither. I'm working."

That does not bode well for Le Corbeau. "All work? No play?"

"Are you calling me a workaholic?" She chastised, her shoulders straightening defensively.

"Absolutely not. Only trying to judge if there's any room for me to help relieve your tension."

"Oh." A flush crept up her cheeks. "You were flirting."

"Should I not be?" I questioned, needing to know if there was a boyfriend I didn't know about.

"No. I mean, yes. I mean —." She cut herself off, that flush deepening. "I'm sorry it's been a while."

"Been a while since you've been flirted with?"

She drew in her bottom lip. The non-verbal answer speaks louder than words. *Fuck.* She's more dangerous as a woman than as a Holst Security employee. She finished her drink way too fast, the alcohol adding to what was already in her system when she was with the other women. With the alcohol-influenced look she gave me, I found her far too tempting to resist. The women she came with were long gone, and I have no idea where she is staying, so stuffing her in a cab is out of the question.

I paid my tab with the bartender, then slipped out of my seat, offering her a hand. She slipped her warm hand into mine as I led her outside and down the street to my hotel. *This is probably a bad idea.* She leaned into me as we walked. The cool air should help clear the fog of alcohol.

Reaching my hotel room, I allowed my little Kitten in first. She let out a soft gasp at the elegance of the room. Living room, bedroom, and terrace. She removed her shoes and then went to the terrace, with a perfect view of the Eiffel Tower. I opened a bottle of water from the mini fridge and poured us each a glass. I took a moment to stare. *She is gorgeous.* The night lights of Paris created a glow around her.

"Beautiful." She sighed, leaning on the balcony and staring at the Eiffel Tower.

"Extraordinarily."

She looked over her shoulder, catching me staring at her. "I meant the tower."

"I know." I offered her the water. "And I meant you."

Blushing, she tried to hide it in the drink I offered. "You don't know me."

"True, but —."

She peered at me expectantly, the glazed look slowly fading. The water and cool night air aid her clarity. She stared at me with those hazel eyes; hesitancy showed in their depths as she waited for me to continue. *What has made you so cautious?*

"I want to learn." I told her truthfully.

"How much?"

"Everything."

I want to touch her. I need to touch her. Slowly raising my hand, I brushed the back of my knuckles against her cheek to the back of her neck and leaned in for a kiss. Kitten placed a hand on my chest, halting my descent to her lips. *Don't push me away now. Not when I'm so close.*

"There's something you should know." She stated, watching me carefully for a reaction. "I have a hectic work life back home which doesn't give me much time for a relationship. Or rather, it gives me no time for a relationship."

"Home is miles away." I reminded her. "Paris is now."

I watched as she thought it over. I pulled my hand back to brush my thumb along her cheek, waiting for her response. The last thing I want is to pressure her into something she doesn't want. However, letting her go might be difficult after our two fireworks-worthy encounters. Her lips parted as she looked up at me, her gaze softening as she came to a decision.

"One night of pleasure won't kill me. If we meet again in this city, then maybe we are meant to have a fling."

We are meant to be more. "Very well."

With that ultimatum and challenge, I took her lips. Going slow, knowing she's still hesitant. The glasses were placed on the wide balcony edge, allowing me to cup her face with both hands. Finally, Kitten opened her mouth for me, her arms wrapping around my neck. My hands trailed down her sides, cupping her ass and lifting her onto the balcony edge. Immediately she spread her legs and hooked them around my waist, drawing me closer. *This woman is a drug.* One kiss, and I know I will want so many more from her.

Her hands slid over my shoulders, pushing the sports jacket off, then worked on the buttons of my shirt. With my shirt open, her fingers played along my chest, feeling every inch of the muscles I've toned over the years. I pulled her t-shirt over her head, revealing a pink cotton bra — a pleasant surprise. I never considered her a pink person. She shivered as I stared.

"Beautiful."

I caught the blush on her cheeks as she squirmed over the compliment. I pushed the cup covering one breast and ducked down, taking the nipple in my teeth. My hand messaged her other breast as my mouth worked the nub to a hardened peak. She moaned and squirmed, her hands in my hair, pressing me to her. *I need more.* Reluctantly I detached my mouth from her breast. Lifting her in my arms, I carried her inside. My little Kitten leaned back just enough to unhook her bra. The contraption fell to the floor somewhere in the living room area.

Once in the bedroom, I shut the door with my foot and placed her on the bed. As she was kind enough to free her breasts, my mouth latched onto the other one I didn't get to taste before bringing her inside. My hands worked on unfastening her jeans. I burned with a need to mark her skin. I kissed and nipped down her body. Then, reaching the waistband, I stood back to strip her of the clothes and could only stare.

"What?" She questioned.

Embarrassment, or maybe it was self-consciousness that set in, she tried to cover herself from my view. *Oh, no, you don't.* My cock responded with the beauty that lay before me in pink cotton underwear. I stripped out of my slacks so that we were on even footing. No, I need her to feel like she has total control. I pulled the briefs off, my cock at full attention. Kitten licked her lips.

"Do you realize how beautiful you are?"

"I'm nothing special." She drew in her bottom lip, a blush gracing her cheeks.

"Look at what you do to me." I gripped my painfully hard cock, pumping it as I spoke. "I'll show you just how special you are."

She sucked in a ragged breath, eyes on my hand. "Do you have a condom?"

Fuck! Not exactly an essential item when packing for a business trip.

"No." I admitted joining her on the bed. "But there are other ways to worship you."

Dipping my head, I kissed her inner thigh. She shivered, then gasped as my mouth covered her mound. Pulling back only long enough to pull those pink panties off, I dived back in. She spread her legs wide, welcoming me into her sex and moaning as my tongue flicked inside her. She twisted her fingers in my hair and lifted her hips. She did everything possible to draw me in deeper.

Whoever made her think she's not special is a fucking idiot. Having her in my bed is one step closer to heaven. Seeing a sliver of vulnerability from my little Kitten gutted me. Tonight, I'll do everything possible to have her wanting to come back. I'll pleasure her until she believes she's beautiful and special. Next time I'll be prepared to bury myself deep inside her warm core and bring her to heaven with me. *This woman is mine.*

Chapter Five

Darcie

I looked at the man still sleeping beside me — the man with stunning blue eyes. Embarrassment crept over me. *I can't believe I slept with a stranger.* Needing to escape before he woke up and realized his mistake, I slipped carefully out of bed. Most of my clothing was in the bedroom, but I couldn't find a few pieces. *Where is my shirt? Where is my bra?* I questioned myself, eyes taking in every inch of the bedroom. Then I remembered this all started on the terrace.

The view of the Eiffel Tower is just as beautiful in the morning as it is at night. I stood on the terrace for a minute too long as I took in the view. Then, shaking my head, I re-entered the hotel room, pausing to glance at the bedroom as I made my way to the door. Impulsively I wrote down my cell phone number on a notepad by the hotel phone. *No, this is just a drunken one-night stand for him.* I ripped the page off the pad, stuffing it in my pocket.

As quietly as possible, I closed the stranger's hotel room door, went down to the lobby, and out the doors, where I caught a taxi. First, I returned to my hotel to shower and change. Then I took another taxi to Marie's, where I left my rental last night.

"Bonjour Darcie." Marie greeted as she exited her house.

"Morning." I smiled at her. "How's Veronica holding up?"

"She seemed very happy about leaving you at the café last night." She offered a knowing smile, which was quickly replaced by a frown. "Mais, elle a pleuré toute la nuit."

Of course, she cried. I felt guilty not being here with my best friend after she lost her husband. I should have ignored the drink the stranger had ordered to lure me away from our table. I shouldn't have caved to Veronica's prodding about going over to talk to him. I should have run after them when I realized they'd left me alone at the café with the stranger.

"I shouldn't have left her last night."

"Ce n'est pas ta faute." Marie tried to abolish my guilt.

"How can I call myself a friend when I leave her in this time of need for some stranger."

"A hot stranger."

I laughed despite myself. "Yes, a hot stranger."

"You got her out of jail. It is more than I could have done."

"Yes." I agreed absently. "Oh, I'm sorry, you were on your way to work. Can you let me know when Detective Giome has the case file on the robbery?"

Marie looked uncertain but nodded anyway. Seeing as my rental blocked hers, I hopped in and backed out of the driveway so she could head off to work. Re-parking in the driveway, I then made my way into the house. Marie had left it unlocked when I arrived, knowing I would be entering to see Veronica. I found my best friend in the kitchen, watching the coffee machine work. She looked lost.

"Make me a cup too."

She jumped at my voice. Then, turning, she forced a smile. "Enjoy your night?"

I pulled her into a hug. "I am so sorry I wasn't here for you last night."

Veronica hugged me back tightly. "I pushed you toward the hot guy. I would have felt guilty if you had come home with me and left him at the café."

I pushed her back, keeping a grip on her shoulders. "Instead, I feel guilty going with him."

"So, he was bad?"

The coffee machine beeped, signalling its brewing completion. I plugged in my cell phone to charge before pouring myself a cup of coffee, doctoring it to perfection with sugar and a touch of cream, then joined Veronica at the tall breakfast bar. Veronica held her coffee in both hands and stared at the caramel-coloured liquid.

"He was bad, wasn't he?"

"I never said that."

She looked up, eyes wide. "Details, woman."

"He's quite pleasant to talk to." I took a moment to sip my coffee before offering her a devilish grin. "He's a devil with his tongue."

"Oh, my, God." She squealed. "Did you get a name? Will you see him again? Come on, Darce, don't leave me in suspense. I have to know every little detail."

"We kept it anonymous. This was just a one-time thing. It's not like I'm going to see him again."

"Really? Why not?"

"One night stand with a stranger is plenty."

Veronica frowned, pity clear in her eyes. "You deserve someone good in your life."

I winced. "Why don't you go get showered and changed? Then, we can go for some therapy shopping."

I watched Veronica hop off the chair and make her way upstairs. I stared down into my coffee. She didn't mean to, but she brought up the memories of Phillip. The man who broke my self-confidence regarding long-term relationships with men. *Bastard.* I should be well over him by now. It's been five years.

Phillip and I met when one of Holst Security's clients died the day we were supposed to start our contract. He was the detective assigned to the case. He flirted relentlessly and asked me out once the case was closed. Phillip was a charmer. The first few months with him were good, really good. Then he began to show his true darker colours. Slowly, so I didn't notice it right away. I chopped it up to stress at work when he lashed out at me. We had been together for over a year when I caught him with his pants down with another woman.

Tristan, being an exceptional partner, hates Phillip for how he treated me. Veronica hates him too. She's received many late-night phone calls during and especially after I broke up with Phillip. It wasn't an easy decision. Eventually, Veronica convinced me to break it off, telling me I deserved someone better. But he still scared me for other men.

My phone chimed. The sound startled me out of my dark thoughts of Phillip. I got up from my seat and headed to where I plugged it in to read the text.

Mystery Person: Morning, beautiful. You left early this morning.

Me: I did.

I answered the text, brows knitting together in confusion. Unfortunately, I didn't recognize the number.

Mystery Person: We could have had breakfast together. In bed. Naked.

Me: Who is this?

Mystery Person: Forget me already? It's only been a few hours since you left my hotel room.

I smiled at the text.

Me: I didn't leave you my number.

Mystery Person: You did. But you have taken the original page. Fortunately, the imprint was left on the next page of the hotel's notepad. I'm glad I got the correct numbers.

Me: I thought you might have regretted last night.

I held my breath for his answer to my confession.

Mystery Person: Never.

His text was quick and confident.

Mystery Person: In fact, I look forward to seeing you again. When I do, I'll get your name.

"What are you smiling about?" Veronica returned. "Is it your hot one-night stand?"

Me: Goodbye, Mr. CEO. I have a hectic day ahead of me.

I didn't wait for a reply as I unplugged the phone and slipped it into my back pocket. "Just Tristan."

She narrowed her eyes suspiciously. To avoid her gaze, I took our mugs to the sink and washed them before we left the house. Veronica used a spare key that Marie gave her to lock up. I slid behind the wheel of the rental car, listening to Veronica's instructions on how to get to her favourite shopping spot.

We spent a few hours weaving in and out of stores, trying on clothes and buying nearly every piece. The trunk of the car filled up fast with the amount we purchased. My credit card bill is going to be high this month. Veronica teared up a few times as certain pieces of clothing reminded her of Paul and how much he would have loved to see her in them. Otherwise, she stayed strong. Being here, with her, is helping a little. *I wish I could do more.*

It was nearing lunchtime when Veronica received a call from a friend inviting her over. We made a quick stop at Marie's to not only drop off her new clothes but so she could change into something new too. She was wearing borrowed clothes from Marie all morning. We then made our way to Veronica's friends' house.

I stared, gaping, at the enormous two-story mansion on the city's outskirts with lots of land. Veronica explained that this friend was a client of Paul's — or at least her husband was. A butler opened the door to a grand entryway.

"Veronica." A strawberry blonde woman called out. "Mon amie."

The two exchanged hugs and kisses on the cheeks. Veronica then turned and pointed me out.

"Josephine Dubois, meet Darcie Manners."

"Darcie!" The woman grabbed my shoulders, kissing both my cheeks. "I have heard so much about you."

Her English is heavy with her French accent. I wasn't quite sure what to say. *What did Vee tell you?* I glanced at Veronica, hoping to see a hint of something to give me an idea of what she's said about me.

"Really?" I replied.

"Oui, bien sûr. Veronica tells tales of her best friend, the security agent. I wondered if they were true — si vous êtes réel."

I laughed hesitantly. "I'm sure whatever she's told you is a fish tale."

"Fish tale? Qu'est-ce que c'est?"

"Highly exaggerated." I amended my words.

"Ah. Venez, venez." She led us to an ornately decorated parlour room. "I have sandwiches prepared."

Not just sandwiches but soup, cheese, crackers, and little pastries. It was all elegantly set out on a low glass table. Sitting in an overstuffed chair, I picked up a bowl of soup, smelling the rich aromas of earthly mushrooms. It tasted heavenly. *I'll never go back to canned soup again.*

Josephine offered her sympathies to Veronica. She offered her a room in her house and anything else she may need. They chatted in French. I know the language and could mostly follow along. Parisian French doesn't sound more beautiful than the French I hear back home — just smoother. Josephine turned her attention to me, asking me about past jobs that Veronica had previously told her and wanting to learn more about how Veronica and I became friends.

"Madame." The butler interrupted with a bow. "Mr. Lux et Mr. Pinot de Rarity Inc. sont ici."

"Merci Gerald. Envoyez-les à la chambre forte." She turned to us. "Pardon. It slipped my mind these gentlemen were coming."

Rarity Inc.? I frowned at that announcement. "What are they appraising?"

Josephine looked stunned that I even knew the company. "Some art and jewels."

"For the auction house?" Veronica inquired. "May we see?"

"Bien sûr."

Josephine led us upstairs, explaining how the auction house has been part of the family for generations. She runs the business while her husband travels the world to find the pieces for her to sell. Then, they use Rarity Inc. to appraise the pieces or restore any that require repair.

The room she led us to was decorated in dark wood with only a desk and couch for its furniture. Sitting on the couch, with its back to the door, sat the two men from Rarity Inc. Two men I recognized as they stood to greet Josephine — both surprised to see me.

"Is that?" Veronica whispered.

"Yep." I whispered back.

"Miss Manners!" Marcus Lux grinned widely.

"Mr. Lux." I smiled politely.

"Marcus." He corrected. "This is quite a surprise."

"Indeed."

He gestured to the man beside him. "Allow me to introduce Killian Pinot."

"Charmed." Killian took my hand, kissing the back.

Mr. CEO practically purred the single word, and the smile he threw me tightened my insides. *How is this possible? Paris is so big.*

"You know them, Darcie?" Josephine questioned, surprised.

"Our paths have crossed." I answered vaguely.

"Gentlemen, this way."

Both men turned their attention to Josephine as she walked over to the long wall. Opening a small hidden panel, she punched in a code that activated the long wall to open up and reveal another room — a safe. Inside were art pieces along the walls, jewels on stands and pillows, stone busts, and vases. Marcus and Killian adorned white gloves and began their inspection.

"How did you come across Rarity Inc.?" Josephine leaned against the desk as Veronica, and I took the couch.

"Yes." Veronica took hold of my hand eagerly. "Do tell."

"Not much to tell. Marcus and Rarity Inc. happen to cross paths with a job." I answered vaguely.

"Come on, Darce, there has to be more."

"There's nothing else I'm willing to say."

"Did you and Marcus have something?" Veronica grinned, teasing me. "And your mystery man from last night, Killian. Did you know they worked together?

"Mystery man?" Josephine questioned.

"Killian was at a café last night, the same one Marie, Darcie, and I went to." Veronica leaned in. "She spent the night with him. Though they didn't know each other's names — until now."

"Je comprends."

"You've been holding out on me, Darce."

"Nope." I stood. "I am so not doing this now, Vee."

I made my way over to the brightly lit safe. My eyes darted between both Killian and Marcus. Killian was examining a stone bust while Marcus was scrutinizing an art piece. I saun-tered over to Marcus.

Marcus smiled at me. "What were you ladies talking about?"

"Nothing I'll tell you about." I looked at the canvas. "Is this really worth anything? It just looks like paint splatter."

He laughed. "It's worth a hundred million dollars."

"Seriously?"

"Yep. It's a Jackson Pollock."

Ridiculous. My eyes drifted over to Killian. He reminded me of Le Corbeau as he examined a necklace. I sidled over to him as he placed it back onto a stand. The chain held a single ruby with gold filigree surrounding it, hanging on a string of pearls.

"A beautiful piece." I commented. "What can you tell me about it?"

He smiled warmly at me. "I won't get into anything techni-cal. I'd say this piece was worn by Queen Mary the First."

"Queen Mary of Scots?"

His smile widened. "Queen Mary wore pieces that rested high on her chest. Like Queen Elizabeth the First, most royalty at the time wore longer pearls because their clothing covered them to their necks."

"I thought they mostly wore pearls back then."

"Mostly." Killian nodded. "But their jewellery boxes held other gems too."

"What about this piece?" I stepped over to the sapphire and diamond necklace.

"Another piece of Queen Mary's." He leaned in to whisper. "It would look beautiful on you."

If Le Corbeau is here, in Paris, he'd go for these pieces. *If he's here, I could use these to trap him.* Killian left me at the

Sapphire as he went to talk to Marcus. My phone chimed. I reviewed the text from Marie and felt my stomach drop.

"Marie." I answered her call when it came in shortly after the text.

"Did you get the picture?"

I left the safe room, heading out to the hall for privacy. "I did."

"Nicholas has the file on the robbery. I found that on his desk." She explained in whispered tones. "C'est important?"

"I'm coming to the station to have a better look."

"Darcie?"

"I don't have an answer for you, Marie. At least not right now." I hung up just as everyone came out of the room.

Veronica took one look at me and frowned. "What's wrong, Darce?"

"I have to go. Can you make it back to Marie's?"

"Gerald can drive her." Josephine announced.

"Thank you."

"Wait! Darcie!" Veronica called after me. "What is going on?"

"Nothing you need to concern yourself with."

I hopped into the rental, making my way to the station as fast as possible. Marie waited for me to sign the visitor's log before taking me upstairs. Desks were grouped in two or three, and men in and out of uniform were busying themselves around the space. Marie led me to Detective Giome's desk, where the man sat pouring over scattered papers.

I took a seat in the empty chair next to his desk. "You have the file on the robbery for me?"

The man scowled, handing over the same image Marie texted. "Who left that?"

"A thief."

"FBI sent their best." He replied dryly.

I bristled at his tone but was careful not to get Agent Moore in trouble with my reply. "I am the best. Where is the rest of the file?"

"I'm reading it. Tell me about the thief that left that."

I took a better look at the picture in my hands. A close-up image of Le Corbeau's calling card shows it was placed carefully on top of a pool of blood. *That's not right.* I took the original calling card that the thief snuck down my shirt from my phone case. I don't know why I felt the need to carry it with me, but I'm glad I did. A strange feeling of relief washed over me.

"It's not him."

"Quoi?"

At Detective Giome's question, I realized I had spoken out loud. "Are you done reading the file?"

He gathered the papers into a file and handed it to me. "Ici."

I returned the calling card and then began reading. Or I tried to, at least. As it is all in French with words I don't understand, I glanced at Detective Giome. *He won't help me.* I looked for Marie. She'd be kind enough to translate. Her desk wasn't too far away either. I could barely see her behind mounds of files. I asked Detective Giome for directions to the washroom. He didn't seem to notice that I took the file with me. Once in the washroom, I texted Marie to meet me there.

"Is everything all right?" She whispered.

"I need help translating this case file." I whispered back.

"Ask Nicholas."

I scoffed. "He already doesn't want me here. I won't give him more reason to hate my presence."

She twisted her fingers together as she decided what to do. *Come on, Marie.* I mentally urged.

"This is about the robbery, not about the murder." I insisted.

Determination formed in her gaze. Using the sink vanity, we opened the file. Papers from the crime scene had slipped in during Detective Giome's rush to hand me the file. Marie hesitated. I pulled out a typed report and asked her to translate it while I examined the pictures within the file. The report stated that only one item was taken from the safe, but they are unsure what it is. The fake calling card was indeed placed neatly on the desk.

I thanked Marie, waiting for her to leave before I called Agent Moore. "Can you leave a message for Le Corbeau?"

"Of course, Darcie. What's the message?"

"Just leave a message that I need to talk and leave him my number."

"What can you tell me about the case?" He questioned.

"The calling card is a fake. But, unfortunately, if no one has seen the original, they could easily think it's real."

"But you have."

"I have." I smiled. "Le Corbeau leaves the card in place of whatever jewel he's stolen. In this case, it was placed neatly on top of a pool of blood."

"Which indicates it was planted. Even if the victim had the card either in his hands or placed on his desk after discovering it, it should have been covered by the blood."

"That's what I thought."

"Good work Darcie." He praised. "Now you'll need to figure out who knows Le Corbeau's calling card. Who would benefit from framing our thief?"

"I thought I'd ask the thief directly."

"You're going to bring him in on the case?" He questioned incredulously.

"Not exactly." I winced. "I hoped to convince him to tell me what I wanted to know. Like, who could frame him? And, does he know what was stolen?"

There was a pause. "Be careful, Darcie. Your plan could easily backfire."

"Do you think it'll be worthwhile for me to gain access to the crime scene?"

"Do you think you will see something that local police missed?"

"Maybe." I shrugged. "I don't know."

"I leave the decision up to you." Typing could be heard in the background. "Your message has been sent. Once he reads it, I should be able to narrow in on his location a little more."

"Thank you, Agent Moore."

"Kent, please."

Chapter Six

♥

Le Corbeau

Darcie. I overheard her friend call her that. My little Kitten has such a pretty name — one she technically hasn't told me. So, as thrilled as I am at learning her name, I'm more concerned about what's going on in that head of hers. She seemed generally intrigued by Queen Mary's jewels until she received that phone call.

Marcus and I didn't stay at Josephine's much longer after Darcie had left. My mind was on my hazel-eyed woman. I want to know why she left in a hurry. Marcus and I parted ways to separate rooms on the same hotel floor. I was settling in on the couch, searching for a movie to watch, when there was a knock on the door.

"Marcus?"

"We have a problem."

"What kind of problem?" I allowed him entry.

He set the laptop he brought onto the coffee table and sat down. "I was just entering a report from today's appraisal when a pop-up about Queen Mary's jewels appeared."

"What kind of pop-up?" Apprehension twisted my gut.

"Someone sent out a request for them."

Not good. "Has anyone responded?"

"Unfortunately."

"Who?"

"Jean Patrice."

Fuck! I wasn't planning on stealing anything while in Paris, but I'll have to now. Before I could think about this problem, my phone received a notification about activity on Darcie's laptop. It was too much of a coincidence to be happening right now for me to ignore. Going to my room, I pulled the laptop out of the suitcase. A message was left in a note program: call me, with her number attached.

"I have to go out for a bit."

"What's going on, Killian?"

"I'm not sure." I answered him honestly. "I have a few calls to make. But, in the meantime, I need you to set up a heist. We cannot let Jean Patrice get his greedy hands on those jewels."

He tossed me a suspicious look but didn't argue. I asked the concierge where the nearest pharmacy was located, then went there. While at the pharmacy, I picked up a box of condoms for the next time Darcie was in my bed. Come hell or high water, I will get her there. The disposable phone was immediately activated and used.

"Who is this?" Darcie questioned cautiously when she answered my call.

"Hello Kitten." I cooed into the phone.

"Corbeau." She sighed in relief. "I see you received my message."

"How did you know I'd see it?"

"Where are you, Corbeau?" She ignored my question.

I smiled. "Does it matter?"

"Yes."

"Paris."

"When?" Her voice tightened.

"A couple of days ago."

"Does the name Paul Laplume mean anything to you?"

"Vaguely." I went through a mental catalogue of names. There are too many for me to remember where I heard that name. "I can look it up in my database and get back to you."

"That would be appreciated." I could picture her drawing in her bottom lip. "Paul has been murdered, and a copycat of your calling card was left at the scene."

Fuck! "It wasn't me, Kitten. I don't condone murder."

"I know it wasn't you. But it still doesn't look good."

"Are you worried about me?" I teased, needing to lighten the mood between us.

"No." She answered too quickly to be believable. "I just don't believe you should be arrested for a crime you didn't commit."

She cares. "How do you know all this?"

"I, too, am in Paris."

"Are you following me now, my little Kitten?"

"I am not here for you." She growled defensively, then hung up.

Double fuck! Rushing back to the hotel, I tossed the name Laplume at Marcus. Thankfully, he was still in my room. Using both our laptops, we looked up the name. I found articles about the murder online. Marcus was searching for his name in connection to any jewel.

"Purple Onyx." Marcus turned his laptop my way. "It's on our watch list, but we haven't heard anything about someone wanting it stolen."

"That's why the name sounded so familiar."

"Why are we looking this up?"

"The owner, Paul Leplume, has been murdered." I showed him the articles. "And an attempt at my calling card was left behind."

Marcus frowned. "How do you know this?"

"Darcie."

"How does she know?"

"She didn't say."

His lips thinned. "She's dangerous, Killian."

I know that. "There's nothing you need to be concerned about."

"Really? She pretended to steal information from our company. Then she suddenly shows up at Josephine's. Now, she's telling you a murderer has left behind a copy of your calling card." Marcus paused. "I don't like it."

"Marcus."

"No, Killian. This woman is going to ruin us. She's just another Thea Stone."

Anger boiled up inside. "Darcie is nothing like Thea!"

"Thea nearly ruined your heist, nearly had you put in jail. Plus, she broke your heart."

"I was young when I met Thea."

Stupid and impressionable.

"And she used you to get the Crystal Owl." He got up. Frustration tightened his muscles as he ran his hands through his brown hair. "Killian, I don't want to see you broken again or get sent to jail."

I have no comeback, no defence against my friend's accusation and worry. Thea and I were thieves just for the fun of it. At the same time, I was trying to build Rarity Inc. — with Marcus. After two years with Thea, she stole the Crystal Owl from me, setting off alarms on purpose to aid in her escape. I was going to ask her to marry me once we finished that heist — but I never saw her again. She broke me. I'd probably be a bitter shut-in if it weren't for Marcus or Rarity Inc. Only three years ago, I created Le Corbeau and stole for the protection of the jewels.

"You're right. Darcie could potentially have me sent to jail." I agreed with him.

"I'll admit." Marcus finally turned my way. Worry was still evident in his features, but the frustration lessened. "I found it amusing to see you so flustered after meeting her. You're normally so composed. And she is beautiful, which is a distraction of its own. But, if you string Darcie along, I fear she'll make a real connection to Rarity Inc. and then bring it and you down."

Do I dare tell him? I sighed. "Breaking into her house wasn't my smartest move. She thinks I have a contact at Rarity Inc."

"Shit, Killian."

I hadn't told him about our conversation or her wall. "She doesn't know who it is. Besides, I don't think she can do anything without proof, and I don't plan on giving her any."

"When we get home, we need to go on hiatus until she's given up."

I nodded in agreement. *That would be for the best.* For now, I told him to rest and enjoy Paris. As long as Darcie is aware of Le Corbeau being in Paris, I don't want Marcus anywhere near a heist. I'll deal with Queen Mary's jewels on my own.

He collected his laptop and left. Alone in the hotel room, I got to work trying to figure out who would want the Purple Onyx and who would want to frame me. Unfortunately, my mind went to Thea — especially after the conversation with Marcus — but I kept asking myself why.

I know Marcus is right about Darcie. My head agrees with him. If she gets too close to me, she'll discover I'm Le Corbeau and have me arrested. But my body, and heart, can't let her go. She's intelligent, fun to talk to, and an addiction both in and out of bed. We haven't known each other long; we barely know each other, but I want her, even for a short time.

Chapter Seven

Darcie

Knocking on the hotel door stirred me from slumber. *Who could be knocking on my door?* The next round of knocks came, this time with my name in a voice I recognized. Still groggy, I slogged to the door. Tristan stood on the other side with a smile and a suitcase. *Am I still dreaming?* I rubbed my eyes just to be sure.

"What are you doing here?"

"I overheard a portion of Agent Moore's conversation with you yesterday and demanded details. Then I went to the boss pleading my case to help you." He held out his hands. "Here I am."

"How did you know where to find me?" I opened the door wider for him to enter.

"Credit card transaction for this hotel and a really nice clerk who helped me surprise my girlfriend."

I frowned. "Girlfriend?"

He shrugged, taking a seat on the extra bed. "I thought a story about some romantic gesture would get me your room number."

"I'm going for a shower." I announced with a shake of my head.

I gathered some clothes and then stepped into the bathroom. I took my time getting ready, the hot water from the shower slowly waking me up. Exiting the bathroom, I found Tristan sitting up against the headboard. *Yep, he's really here.* A small part of me almost hoped he was just a dream.

Tristan immediately requested an update. I made the bed I'd slept in and sat before diving into the story. I told him everything that's happened, from Veronica's time in jail to Paul's murder, Le Corbeau's calling card, and Rarity Inc. being in the city. I explained to him that I was acting as an FBI liaison agent, and because of that, I convinced the local police captain to let me into the crime scene to examine the theft.

Tristan stared at me. "That's a lot in only two days."

"Coming to Paris, my only goal was to get Veronica out of jail."

"Which you accomplished. Now what? Catch Le Corbeau?"

"Well." I trailed off, embarrassed to say I didn't have the next steps. "Honestly, catching the thief on home turf would be much more beneficial. Agent Moore and I thought we should prove he's not Paul's killer."

"Why?"

"Because he's not."

"Darcie." Tristan swung his legs to the side of the bed. Leaning forward, he put his hands on my knees. "You are not here to find Paul's killer."

"I know, and I'm not."

"If you prove Le Corbeau didn't kill your friend's husband, you are then looking for the real killer. You have to let the police do their job."

"Their job had them arresting Veronica." I scowled.

"Darcie, you're obsessed with this thief."

Am I? "I'm not obsessed."

Tristan let out a resigned sigh. "I came here to help. The sooner you finish whatever you're doing here in Paris, the sooner we can return home to our job."

"Detective Giome is meeting me at Veronica's house." I stood to gather the car keys, my phone from its charging place and the small pocketable travel wallet. "If I can figure out what was stolen, it might also be a clue as to who killed Paul. A lead the police can follow up with."

It took just over half an hour to arrive at Veronica's house. I parked in front of a tall thin three-story building. Detective Giome was already there, waiting outside for me. I introduced Tristan and received complaints that I was the only one permitted to enter the crime scene. I couldn't quite catch every word as he spoke in rapid French. *This man is so prickly.* Tristan smiled and explained — far more patiently than I would — how an extra set of eyes won't hurt.

From my little interaction with him at the station, I've noticed he's well-respected among his peers. This situation has lessened my chances of being in Detective Giome's good graces. I need to remain in his good graces to prove Le Corbeau, and Veronica are not killers. Having made a decision, Detective Giome handed us gloves and booties with a growled order for us not to touch anything.

The moment I stepped foot into the house, I regretted never coming to Paris sooner to visit. I could easily picture Paul and Veronica greeting guests in the entryway. Detective Giome took us to the second floor. He explained that the crime scene had remained the same aside from any residue left over from his investigators.

Two walls featured bookcases. One of those walls revealed a safe similar to the one Josephine has, while one wall had windows letting in quite a bit of natural light. The chair was spun away from the desk — dried blood pooled at the chair's base, and a gap revealed where Paul's body sat. *Focus on finding what the thief stole.* I reminded myself and blinked back the tears.

I needed to re-focus my mind on the room as a whole. For starters, by taking a better look at the safe. Inside there were many numbered drawers. Only one of those drawers was open, and the glass protecting whatever was inside was smashed. The keyhole to open the drawer had scratches on it. *The thief clearly can't pick a lock.* Aside from a velvet inside, nothing indicated what was stolen.

"Did anyone discover what was stolen?" I questioned Detective Giome.

"Non."

"The thief didn't know the code to get in." Tristan announced.

"The report did claim it was a forced entry." I joined him outside the safe.

Tristan held two sets of cut wires between his fingers. "Yeah, I'd say this is forced entry. The thief pried off the keypad and cut the wires, short-circuiting the system, which forced the bookcase door to open."

I pointed to the desk. "Detective, were all the drawers searched?"

"Oui. We are not amateurs." Detective Giome responded haughtily.

I believe him, but I have to look for myself. If I have a secret safe with numbered drawers, I'd want a way to record what is in those drawers. The desk's top extended beyond the depth of the drawers, its lip hiding the drawers in shadow. A regular cop would stand in front of the desk and search the visible drawers. Instead, I crouched down to look at the drawers head-on.

"Was this locked one looked at?"

Detective Giome crouched beside me, a frown deepening on his features. "Non."

I ran my fingers over the keyhole before trying to open the drawer with the drawer pull. Locked. I searched all the other drawers to see if a key was tapped to the bottom. No luck. I asked Detective Giome, who had stood back up, to hand me two paper clips. I haven't needed to pick a lock since high school. It took a little time to figure out the correct sequence, then the drawer unlocked quickly. *Like riding a bike.* Inside there was a red leather-bound journal.

"Qu'avez-vous trouvé?" Detective Giome took the book from me.

"I'm not sure what I found exactly." I took the book back from him to flip through it. "Tristan, what is the number on the open drawer in the safe?"

"7091."

I ran my finger down the line of 7080s until I reached 7091. "Purple Onyx."

"C'est tout?" Detective Giome took the book back. "Nothing about whom it belongs to?"

"I don't get it." Tristan admitted. "If you're going to steal something, wouldn't you want the owner to know you have it? Why place a fake calling card from a different thief?"

"Fake?" The detective closed the book. "What are you not telling me?"

"The calling card found is a fake version from a real thief." I explained. "Now that I've seen the room, I can confirm it was also planted to cover the real killer's tracks."

Tristan stared at me. "In all your research, did you find anything that would indicate that someone would want to frame him for revenge?"

"No."

"Vous avez terminé?" Detective Giome interrupted.

"Yes, we're done."

He led us out and locked up the crime scene. I am still trying to figure out where to go from here. Detective Giome is in charge of finding Paul's murderer. Unfortunately, it's been established that the thief I'm after isn't involved in this matter, so I won't be able to pull any more FBI strings.

Tristan took the car keys from me. "What's bugging you?"

"Did we just prove that Le Corbeau isn't the thief and therefore isn't the one who killed Paul?"

"If this were our case, then yes." Tristan answered carefully. "But this isn't our case. So detective Giome could still assume that Le Corbeau is still the killer."

"I don't understand why a fake calling card was left behind." I admitted. "Was it to get away with the theft of the Purple Onyx by blaming someone else? Was it revenge against Le Corbeau?"

"I don't have those answers, Darcie."

"You don't, but Le Corbeau might."

"What did you do?" Tristan asked worriedly.

I shrugged. "I asked Agent Moore to leave a message for Le Corbeau on my laptop. He, um, called me yesterday."

"Darcie." He ground out.

"I already told him about the murder and the fake calling card."

"And?"

"He confirmed he didn't kill Paul, but I didn't get anything else from him."

"Do you honestly think he'd give you a straight answer?"

I sighed and leaned back in my seat. "No, I didn't. I at least hoped he'd look into it."

The tension in the rental car rose. Tristan has always disliked it when I go vigilante like this and do outrageous things by myself before talking them over with him. When working a job, I usually don't have time to go over the plans that form in my head with him. In this case, he's a friend who has come to help me. *Agent Moore's already warned me to be careful.* I'm flying by the seat of my pants on this one. I don't need to prove that Le Corbeau didn't commit this theft, but I feel like I have to. It's not something I can easily explain, nor is it something Tristan would understand. When my phone chimed, I practically jumped out of my seat.

Killian: Care to have dinner?

Killian's text brought a smile to my face.

Me: Love to. I could use a distraction.

Killian: If it's a distraction you need, we can skip dinner.

A pleasurable coursed through me.

Me: Dinner first, Killian.

Killian: Of course, then we can work off the calories later. I will make reservations at a restaurant in the hotel for six.

Me: Dress code?

Killian: Semi-formal?

"What's that about?" Tristan inquired when I put my phone away.

"I, uh." I squirmed. "I met someone the other day."

"He makes you smile."

"He's easy to talk to." I rushed to justify my actions. "It's just a Paris fling. When we return home, we won't see each other again."

He frowned. "Why not? If he makes you smile like this, I think you should keep seeing him. That is unless you don't think he's boyfriend material. Or is it because he's a local."

My turn to frown. "I'm a bad judge of boyfriends."

"You've had one."

"And it turned out horribly."

"Not every man you meet will be like Phillip." He reached over to squeeze my knee. "I know it's delayed, but I'm sorry about Paul and Veronica."

"Thanks. And thank you for coming, Tristan."

"You're my partner and friend. I'm always here for you, Darcie."

Him being here is a comfort, even if there's nothing for us to do. Tristan returned us to the hotel room. There was nothing to do but wait for Le Corbeau to call me with answers. *Who knows when that'll be.* Grabbing the ice bucket, I left the room. I need to move, do something. Speaking to Le Corbeau is the best option. He'd have insight into who'd want to frame him and who'd want the Purple Onyx. The longer I waited for him to call with answers, the more uneasy I became.

When my phone rang, I dug it out of my pocket. An unknown number appeared. The same unknown number Le Corbeau used yesterday. I sucked in a breath. *I hope he's calling with good news.*

"Darcie Manners."

"Kitten." Le Corbeau responded with a smile in his voice.

Finally. I didn't bother with pleasantries and went straight to the point. "What can you tell me about the Purple Onyx."

"Paul Leplume is the last known owner of this rare gem."

"You knew he had it?"

"After our talk yesterday, I looked into it the name. He's had it for the past couple of years, but I haven't heard any whispers about plans to steal it."

"What about you? Is it something you'd steal?"

"There's no need." He stated matter of fact. "Besides, the only thing I want to steal is your heart, Kitten."

Heat rose at the flirtation. "Why isn't there a need for you to steal the Purple Onyx?"

"It's on my watch list, but that's as far as it has made. There are things I must consider before I steal something."

"Such as?" I prompted.

"Who else would want it."

"And who else wanted the Purple Onyx?"

"No idea."

I stuck the ice bucket on the little shelf, using my hip to hold it in place, then pushed the button for the ice. It made an awful amount of noise.

"Can you think of anyone who would want revenge against you? Another thief you've crossed? Someone who might know your signature?"

"What is that sound?" He queried.

"Ice machine. Now, answer the question. Who'd deliberately leave a fake calling card behind to frame you?"

"A few names have crossed my mind since you told me about it yesterday."

"And?"

"None of them are in Paris."

"Well, crap, that led me nowhere." I let out a huff.

"I'll keep digging." Le Corbeau chuckled. "I knew you cared about me, Kitten."

"Not in the slightest." I lied.

I hung up and returned to the room with a full ice bucket. As I went through my suitcase for my date with Killian tonight, I updated Tristan on what Le Corbeau had just told me. *There's nothing here.* All I could find, even within the new bags I'd bought when out with Victoria, were cute tops and jeans. Nothing worth a semi-formal restaurant. I don't even have the right shoes. Giving Veronica a call, I told her of the date and the fashion emergency. She ordered me over to Marie's, so we could go shopping.

Chapter Eight

Le Corbeau

I waited for Darcie in the hotel lobby. She looked stunning. Her brown hair was done in gentle waves, and her makeup was light, highlighting her gorgeous hazel eyes. She wore a knee-length, off-shoulder dress that perfectly accentuated her curves and those heels. Fuck, those heels were a turn-on. They elongated her shapely legs. *Such a temptress.* When she smiled at me, I felt my cock harden. The things I wanted to do to this woman — both in and out of that dress — flooded my mind.

"Hi." She said timidly.

I wrapped an arm around her waist and hauled her against me. The heels raised her lips three inches closer to mine. I kissed her. Deeply. My tongue slid into her mouth to run along hers. When I pulled back, she was breathless in my arms.

"You look ravishing."

She blushed. "Thank you."

Darcie blushed so easily, and I loved seeing the colour on her cheeks. Especially when I put it there. Stepping back, I offered her my arm. She took it with a soft smile.

"I hope you enjoy dinner tonight, Darcie."

She frowned. "I don't recall telling you my name."

"You didn't." I told her. "At Josephine's, I overheard your friend call you by name."

"Oh. Well, I guess you should know it since I know yours. My name is Darcie Manners."

"It's a pleasure to meet you officially, Darcie."

The maître-de took us to a table by a window overlooking an indoor garden. I pulled Darcie's chair out before going around to sit across from her. I didn't want to be so far away. I wanted to sit beside her with my arm over her shoulders and tucked into my side. *It's only the first official date. I should remain gentlemanly.* Darcie frowned as she looked over the menu.

"Can't decide what to eat?" I questioned lightly.

"It all sounds delicious." She shifted in her seat. "I wasn't expecting Asian cuisine."

"Is this not to your liking? There's a lounge here that sells hamburgers."

She shook her head. "It's not that. I like Asian cuisine. It's just unexpected."

A waiter came around asking if we were ready. I looked at Darcie. She smiled and told the waiter what she'd like, in French. I also gave him my order and ordered us a bottle of Riesling. The white wine will pair nicely with the fish we ordered. The waiter nodded and left, returning shortly with the wine. He opened it at the table and poured a little into my glass to try. Once I approved it, he poured Darcie and me a glass and then left us alone again.

"Are you a wine connoisseur?" Darcie teased.

"Not at all." I shrugged. "I much prefer a whiskey when I get home from work or a beer on the weekends."

"Beer, now you're talking my language."

"Do you not drink wine?"

"Of course I do." She took a sip from her glass. "There's a higher chance you'll find beer over a bottle of white wine in my fridge."

"A woman after my own heart." I grinned. "I just want our date to be perfect."

"Nothing is perfect."

"To me, you are." I reached across the table to take her hand.

"I have plenty of flaws." She whispered.

"Name one." I challenged.

Darcie's smile tightened. "I'm obsessive. My partner tells me I'm always trying to prove I'm the best."

"Partner?"

"I work at Holst Security, the private security firm I mentioned the other night. All employees work in teams of two."

"How did your path cross with Marcus?"

"The Eye."

I tried not to react to the gem's name. "Marcus told me the fake Eye we had prepared didn't fool the thief we feared might show."

"Tristan and I were lead on the security team tasked to protect it." Darcie frowned.

She looked like she wanted to say something. *Did I show my hand somehow?* Darcie shook her head and smiled.

"How did you get into the appraisal world?"

The waiter came with our dishes. He verified that we didn't need anything else before leaving.

"My mother used to tell me the history of a ring passed down in our family every night like a bedtime story." I began between bites of dinner. "It piqued my interest in the history of gems and other objects — some found in museums, others in people's homes. Then, when I was about twelve, the ring was stolen. It was then I decided to try and find it for her."

"Have you found the ring?"

"Unfortunately, I have not. I started Rarity Inc. in the hopes of the ring coming to me while, at the same time, I wanted to tell others how precious their items are so they can protect them. The company grew to do restorations as well."

"Do you know anything about the thief? Maybe I can help you find the ring for your mother. I'm really good at research."

I'm well aware of that. In two weeks, from when I first met her at the Museum of Terra to when I broke into her home, she found a lot of information about me. I took her hand in mine, kissing the knuckles.

"That's kind of you, but the police couldn't get any leads back when it was stolen, so there wouldn't be anything for you to look into. Besides, even if the ring is found, my mother would want me to propose with it."

"Okay." She pulled her hand away. "But if you change your mind."

Smiling, I changed the subject slightly. "Did you have anyone influence you into the world of private security?"

"I was a bit of a troublemaker when I was a kid." She grinned sheepishly. "All that changed when I was fourteen. My parents and I were on summer vacation at an all-inclusive hotel when

I met Detective Kyrie Albert. She was so pretty, I wondered why she was alone, so I watched her. I caught her taking secretive phone calls and sly pictures and trying to sneak into off-limits areas. So, I confronted her — that's when she told me who she was."

I laughed. "I can picture a miniature version of you hiding behind hotel decorations and peeking around corners to see what she was doing."

"Turns out." She continued with a playful glare. "She was looking for her husband. He was being held against his will somewhere on the premises. I had begged her to let me help. I was so bored. We became close that summer. I was inspired by how strong-willed and badass she was. When I returned home, I researched how to be a cop because I wanted to be just like her."

"Yet you're not a cop." I pointed out.

Darcie shook her head. "Kyrie helped me get through the police academy. Then, while in uniform, I crossed paths with Holst Security. I didn't feel challenged enough as an officer, so I changed careers. Working with Holst Security reminds me of that summer with Detective Albert."

"Have you kept in contact with this detective?"

Again, she shook her head. "I felt as though I let her down when I switched careers that I couldn't bring myself to reach out to her."

"Maybe I can be next to you when you decide to talk to her?" I offered, wanting a way to guarantee a next time. "For moral support?"

The offer caused her to frown. Darcie was only considering this time in Paris as a fling and had no intention of seeing me when we went home. *I'll change her mind.* She changed the subject, and we continued to learn more about each other throughout dinner. When the table was cleared, I didn't want to let her go and invited her to my room. Darcie politely turned me down, claiming she didn't have sex on the first date.

I laughed. I walked her outside so she could catch a taxi. Before letting her leave, I pulled her into my arms for a scorching goodnight kiss. I want her to regret leaving me or, better yet, change her mind about leaving me. A taxi pulled up, and I pulled away to open the door. She was breathless when she slid into the back seat.

I didn't want to let her go, but it was for the best. I have a heist to do tonight. I could have left Darcie in my bed, asleep and satisfied, then returned to her warm body after the heist. But, unfortunately, it would have drawn questions if she had woken up while I was gone. Questions I don't want her to ask. Letting her go might be smart, but it is certainly not what I want to do.

Josephine's house is the least secure house I've broken into. I picked the lock to the back door. No alarms went off, no one came running, and no guard dogs barked. I carried a portable security camera jammer to scramble the feed on any camera I could pass. Still, I watched my steps and kept my ears open. Finally, I made it to the safe room. Slipping inside, I went to the hidden panel to punch in the code I watched Josephine enter the other day. The secret safe opened, and bright lights from inside starkly contrasted with the room's darkness. My eyes swept over the various objects within.

"Close the door."

I jumped at the unexpected voice. Then, obeying the command, I closed the door, turning with my hands up. I didn't expect to find Darcie here. I certainly didn't expect to see her lying on the only piece of furniture with an arm over her eyes. *Abandoning me for me, how impolite, Kitten.* As the safe closed, the light vanished, leaving us in complete darkness.

"Now, this is unexpected." I put my hands down. "Kitten."

"I'm glad I caught you." I heard her move, my eyes not yet adjusted to the sudden darkness.

"You haven't caught me yet."

She stood directly in front of me and frowned. "I needed to see you."

My heart soared at her statement, but it was a complicated feeling. We were just on a date together. Yet here she is, telling another man she needed to see him. She doesn't know I'm the same man she left at the hotel. So I played into her unknown, flirting with her. I wrapped an arm around her waist and pulled her to me.

"I knew it." I teased. "You do care for me."

"Let me rephrase that." She placed her hands on my chest as if to push away but didn't. "I wanted to see your reaction when I ask you some questions."

"Ask away."

Why isn't she fighting me? What angle is she playing? I need to be careful. She tricked me into breaking into her house last time. Now she's here. I feel like I'm always a step behind her.

"What can you tell me about the Purple Onyx?" Darcie stared into my eyes as she asked the question.

"It belongs to Paul Laplume."

"Belonged." She corrected. "The Purple Onyx is gone."

That changes things. I made a mental note to look into the current whereabouts of the gem. Few people wanted it.

"Purple Onyx is gone?" I verified.

"Yes."

"I didn't take it."

She bit her bottom lip. I cupped her chin, then gently pulled her lip out with my thumb.

"Kitten, what is going on in that pretty mind of yours?"

"I'm wondering, if the Purple Onyx is found, then maybe it will lead to Paul's killer."

I smiled. "Are you asking me to steal for you?"

She shook her head. "Not steal, only track."

"And what would I get for my efforts?"

She raised herself on her toes, brushing her lips softly against mine. "I won't have you arrested for breaking into Josephine's."

There's that. This woman is confusing. I feel like she's flirting with Le Corbeau even after our pleasant date. Has she put the pieces together? Or is she just using her feminine charm to throw me off balance? Part of my brain is telling me to run, that this is a trap. But most of the blood has gone south, and the need to kiss her is far too tempting for me not to take this opportunity.

"Corbeau?" She looked up at me, brows knitting together. Her fingertips grazed along my mask. "What are you thinking?"

I'm thinking about you. Cupping the back of her neck, I pressed my lips firmly against hers. The need to kiss her was too overwhelming to ignore. She gasped, hands tightening in my shirt, and I held her close. Parting her lips to deepen the kiss, a soft moan slipped out, and she leaned into me. *That's it, Kitten, give in to temptation.* She untangled her hands, placed them firmly on my shoulders and pushed back, but only enough to separate from our kiss. I trailed my lips along her neck and shoulders, leaving little kisses on her exposed skin.

"You can't." Her voice came out shaky. "Kiss me." I nibbled a spot on her neck which awarded me a moan. "Like that."

"Why?" I trailed kisses along the neckline of her dress.

"Because."

"You can't deny there's something between us." I argued.

"It's called the law."

A chuckle rumbled through me as I came up to meet her gaze. "I was thinking of clothes. They have got to go."

"Corbeau." She ground out.

"Kitten."

"This isn't right."

"You're right. A bed will be far more comfortable than a couch."

"I'm dating someone."

"I'm more fun." I held her tighter, knowing she was talking about me, but I couldn't resist teasing her.

Darcie took in a shaky breath as a beautiful blush coloured her cheeks. "You didn't kill Paul — but someone is trying to frame you."

Talk about throwing an ice bucket on the situation. "Why must you bring that up now? Things were just about to get hotter between us."

"We're not meant to be." She frowned. "Can you think of anyone who would want to frame you? Someone who would want revenge? Someone who knows your calling card?"

"I've been compiling a list since we last spoke."

"Send me the list." Again, she pushed, and this time I let her go.

"I don't want you going anywhere near the people on this list."

"You don't have a say in my life choices."

"They are dangerous people." I argued. "Where are Queen Mary's jewels? I see you're not wearing them this time."

"How observant." She rolled her eyes. "I had Josephine move Queen Mary's jewels before you got here. So they will be safe until the auction."

I frowned. *Stubborn woman.* "That wasn't very smart of you, Kitten. Where are they?"

"I'm not telling you."

"Damn it!" I growled, running my hands through my hair. "You have no idea what you just did."

"I protected precious jewels from a thief like you."

"Wrong." I don't have time to explain it to her. Marcus and I will have to come up with a new plan. "You just put them in danger."

Chapter Nine

♥

Darcie

Stupid thief. Stupid body. I reacted the same way to Le Corbeau as I do when Killian kisses me. I felt all tingly and safe. Either I was just needy after abruptly leaving my date, or there's something about Le Corbeau that I'm missing.

Come morning, I called Tristan for a pickup. While I waited, I updated Josephine about the near theft. She was horrified that my late-night hunch was accurate. Paranoid, she begged me to go to the auction tonight in case there was another attempt to steal Queen Mary's jewels. I agreed on the condition that Tristan comes as well.

When Tristan picked me up, I informed him of Josephine's request. We took some time to discuss the auction tonight and learned how her current security works. Josephine wanted us to travel with her to the auction house. She'll keep Queen Mary's jewels with her until it is time for the auction. We made plans to return later today.

Once alone in the car, I told Tristan about Le Corbeau's statement about me putting the jewels in danger by not allowing him to steal them. It bugged me all night after he left, irritated.

"That's an odd thing to say." Tristan frowned. "Why would stealing jewels first keep them safe?"

"I have no idea." I crossed my arms, frustrated. "There's so much I don't know."

"Are you going to update Agent Moore?"

"I should."

"Darcie?" Agent Moore questioned when he answered.

I kept the call on speaker. "I have an update."

"Go ahead."

"Le Corbeau did reach out after you'd left that message for him. He doesn't know who framed him. When I told him who was murdered, he looked into it and found that Paul owned a jewel called Purple Onyx. It's the same information Tristan and I discovered when we accessed the crime scene."

"Very good. At least we're on the same page as him."

"Maybe on that matter." I let out a heavy sigh. "I had a hunch he would try to steal Queen Mary's jewels."

"I heard they are up for auction tonight." Agent Moore commented. "How did you hear about it?"

"I know the woman who is selling them. Anyway, my hunch panned out because I could move those jewels before Le Corbeau came to take them. He said something odd that I want to run by you."

"Okay?"

"He said I put them in more danger by not letting him steal them."

"While you've been in Paris, I've been going over Le Corbeau's first couple of thefts with a fine toothcomb and reaching out to the owners of whom he's stolen from." Agent Moore explained. "What was stolen has been returned. I also found other well-known and dangerous thieves looking to steal the items before Le Corbeau got to them. Anywhere from one to two months after knowledge of Le Corbeau's theft has died down and there's no more talk about having the item stolen again, he returns it to the owner, who stays quiet about having it returned."

"That couldn't have been easy to find."

"It wasn't. I've got a friend in the Jewel and Gem Theft division. They've been keeping an eye on a couple of these dangerous thieves. He told me about some dark web, back door chatter on particular pieces. These thieves are unhappy that Le Corbeau constantly beats them to the punch. As a result, they are losing business."

"They could easily want revenge on Le Corbeau." My stomach knotted at the thought of them being in Paris and Le Corbeau not knowing. "They could be behind Paul's murder."

"He's made many enemies, but none are in Paris."

"I guess that's a good thing."

"You've done excellent work, Darcie. When should I expect your return?"

"Tristan and I have been asked to assist in the auction's security tonight." I looked at my partner, who was parking the car at the hotel. "I still want to spend a couple more days with my friend."

"Very well. Stay safe."

Agent Moore hung up. *I really should check in on Vee.* Tristan didn't say anything about the conversation with the FBI agent. When we reached my room, he lay on the bed closing his eyes while I collected fresh clothes and went to the

83

bathroom. Whenever there's a lot of information to process, Tristan closes his eyes to sort through it all.

He's explained it to me once, it's like he can see it all on cue cards in his mind, and it's easier for him to move it around and put the information in the right place. To him, it's a puzzle that needs to be solved. So it's helpful when we're doing a job. He can see the layout in his mind in a 3-D blueprint and visualize the security movements to point out any flaws in a plan.

He'd opened his eyes when I came out of the bathroom. I raised a brow in question, wondering what his mind had been able to sort through. He shook his head and explained that there were too many unknowns to figure out who'd want to frame Le Corbeau. I felt as though he was holding something back. *He'll tell me when he's ready.* I grabbed the car keys and told him I wanted to see Veronica. He smiled and joined me. Veronica and Tristan haven't officially met yet, but I've told them enough stories about each other that they should get along just fine.

"Tell me about your night." Veronica urged as she poured coffee for all of us.

"Not much to tell." I shrugged. "Dinner was fantastic, conversation informative."

"Did you spend the night with him?"

I shook my head. "I spent the night at Josephine's."

Her brows knitted. "Why?"

"I had a gut feeling there was going to be a robbery."

Tristan scoffed at my answer, which rewarded him with a glare. Veronica passed over the cups of coffee along with cream and sugar.

"And?" Veronica pressed.

"And I was right. The thief came and left with nothing thanks to me."

She deflated. "You are so boring. You could have spent the night with a hot CEO who has taken an interest in you — instead, you leave him to ensure a robbery doesn't happen."

"What's wrong with that?" I countered.

"Sometimes I miss the old you. The one who bent the rules a little to have fun. I think you've lost a part of yourself after the academy."

"Wait." Tristan interrupted. "Darcie Manners used to bend the rules?"

"She was actually fun." Veronica nodded.

"Hey!" I felt offended by that statement. "I'm still fun."

My best friend ignored me. "We used to go dancing and skip school to see a movie. But, of course, my parents didn't like her too much, thought she was a bad influence."

"Yet you're still friends." Tristan pointed out.

"Of course." Veronica smiled brightly. "Darce was always there when I needed her."

"I have to ask; did she pick locks when she was younger?"

"How else was she supposed to get into a locked classroom to slip her late assignment into the grading pile?"

A grin spread across his face. "Wow. I'm learning so much."

I frowned at them. *Have I really changed that much?* Sure, I've cut back on going out with friends, and dating isn't exactly a priority — especially after Phillip. So, I let my partner and best friend swap stories about me while I got lost in my thoughts. It brought a smile to Veronica's face, which halted any complaint I may have raised.

I thought about Le Corbeau and that kiss he gave me last night. I sipped my coffee slowly. That blue-eyed thief is a dangerously good kisser. *Blue eyes.* Killian also has blue eyes. It could be a coincidence that the two men who make my knees go weak with a kiss have the same colour eyes. *Maybe they are the same person.* A cold chill trickled down my spine. There are so many implications with that thought.

"Darcie?" Tristan's voice penetrated my thoughts.

"Hmm? What?"

"I asked if you wanted to go sightseeing today."

I looked at Veronica. "You want to go?"

She shook her head. "I'm going to visit Paul's family."

"Do you want me to go with you?"

"I need to do this myself."

I nodded in understanding. "Call me if you need anything."

Veronica hugged me tight. "I know."

With that, she ushered us out of the house. Tristan slipped behind the wheel of the rental car.

"Care to tell me what's on your mind?"

"Not particularly."

"Very well." He shrugged. "Where to first?"

"You choose."

Tristan took us first to the Eiffel Tower, where we made our way to the top. The aerial view of the city was breathtaking, and the air seemed so fresh, but that could have just been my imagination. I swear I could see Killian's hotel from here, which didn't help my current mental dilemma about him. Tristan stayed by my side, pointing out other famous spots we could visit. Unfortunately, our plans were cut short as Marie texted me an address inviting me for lunch. Shortly after, Killian called asking the same thing, which I turned down — Marie asked first. Besides, I want to figure out how I feel about him potentially being Le Corbeau before I see him again.

Tristan drove me to a Chinese restaurant. Marie waited outside for me. I invited him to join, but he claimed he would continue sightseeing. My gut told me he was lying. *I wonder what he's really going to do.*

"This place is a little far from the station. Is the Chinese food really that good?" I questioned, staring at the façade.

"No idea." She shrugged. "I know I shouldn't have, but I used Veronica's phone and the 'find my friend' app. Paul has frequently been going to two places. So when I went to work, I looked them up. The first is a casino — I checked it out this morning, and he's been spending lots and losing it all. The second is this restaurant."

"So, you called me to check it out with you?"

"Nicholas caught me looking into this place and warned me away. Il y a quelque chose ici."

I like this side of her. "Then let's figure out what it is."

We were led to a table and given an order sheet. It was dim sum style where we order several items, then the waiter takes the sheet to the kitchen then brings the table everything ordered as it's made. Thankfully, I could recognize quite a few things and ordered what I wanted. I looked around. The restaurant wasn't bustling for lunchtime.

Her eyes widened as she stared past my shoulder. "That's why Nicholas warned me away."

"Look away." I ordered.

"Trop tard." Wide, scared eyes turned to me. "He's coming over."

"Mesdames." A man stopped at our table.

"Bonjour." I looked up at him. Dark, slicked-back hair, dis-arming smile, well-tailored suit — warning signals rang in my head. *Stay calm, Darcie.* "Can we help you sir?"

"Foreigners." He took a chair from another table and sat at ours. "Welcome to my restaurant. If there's anything you need, anything at all, don't hesitate to ask."

"Then, could you please get us some water?"

He laughed. "Of course."

"Breathe, Marie." I whispered when he left. "Who is he?"

"Jean Patrice." She hissed, panicked. She didn't expect to see him, and he frightened her.

"Here you are." He placed the water down, along with himself, at the table. "Is there anything else I can get you? Spring rolls? Wonton soup? A confession for a crime I didn't commit?"

That caught me off guard. *What a strange thing to say.* Marie understood. Her breath caught as she looked up at him, shocked.

I spoke calmly, drawing his gaze my way. "We're just here for lunch."

On cue, our food began to arrive.

"You, I don't recognize." He pushed my hair off my shoulder, gripping the back of my neck. "A word of warning, ma belle — not all the police in this city are trustworthy."

I smiled at him. "How would a restaurant owner know that?"

His lips twisted into a smile. "I like you. What's your name?"

"My name is not interested, and you can reach me at 1-800-let me go."

Again, he laughed, putting both hands up defensively. "Have a good lunch, ladies."

Marie looked far too shaken to eat. I was more irritated. In whispered tones, I got Marie calm enough to eat something. It both smelled and tasted delicious. I went to pay for lunch when the man, Jean Patrice, offered to do so. There was no way I would be in debt to a stranger. I declined the offer. He handed me his business card, hoping we'd cross paths again. I glanced at it, then left it on the counter. *I hope not, Jean Patrice.*

Once in Marie's car, I demanded to know who Jean Patrice was and why she was so scared of him. She explained that he's a well-known — extremely dangerous — loan shark with plenty of powerful men in his pocket. He's been linked to various crimes, but nothing ever sticks. But, unfortunately, too many who work for him take the fall and refuse to give him up.

"If Paul has been coming here, he must have been borrowing money to gamble at the casino." I stated.

"Looks that way."

"Will Detective Giome look into this?"

"Non."

"Why not?"

She gulped, hands tightening on the steering wheel. "It is rumoured that the last cop who went after Jean Patrice had his family murdered."

I paled. "Shouldn't that be even more reason to put him behind bars?"

"Without concrete evidence, no one dares to go after Jean Patrice. He's far too dangerous. I believe there are too many cops that have their pockets lined with his money."

I nibbled my bottom lip. If this man has anything to do with Paul's murder and the framing of Le Corbeau, he can't just be allowed to walk free. *Does Corbeau know him? Can Agent Moore help?* Marie drove me to the station so she could go back to work. I then called Tristan, asking him to pick me up. I want to go over this new piece of evidence with him. And we need to prepare for the auction tonight.

Chapter Ten

♥

Le Corbeau

Marcus, as I predicted, was furious that I returned empty-handed. He would not stop berating me about my failure, about Darcie, or about how we're going to get our hands on Queen Mary's jewels now. I have some ideas on getting those jewels, but Marcus is too wound up to hear anything. *How did she know I'll be there last night?* I went through every conversation we had, trying to figure out if something had slipped. Nothing came to mind. Nothing said between us or in our texts would have revealed anything.

Marcus took the morning to himself, needing to be away from me as he processed all the bad news I dumped on him at breakfast. I couldn't blame him. I wasn't too pleased over my failure either. I needed to know if I slipped up somehow. If I invite Darcie for lunch, I might be able to pry any information she has on me.

"Good morning Darcie."

"Killian." Her tone sounded a little cold.

"I was hoping you'd do me the honour of joining me for lunch."

"I already have plans. Another time."

With that, she hung up. I stared at my phone. Something is wrong. Not knowing if she turned me down because she genuinely has other plans or if it has something to do with Le Corbeau has me nervous. But then, there was a knock on the door.

"I'm still pissed at you." Marcus stated when I let him in. "But we need to get those jewels."

"We're going to the auction." I told him. "We'll offer our services to whoever buys them, giving us a new opportunity. Or we can have someone buy them for us, and then we can meet up for them to be handed over."

Marcus stared at me. "And what sucker is going to buy something he can't keep?"

"I don't know, but it can't be anyone connected to Rarity Inc."

"Killian, having someone buy the pieces for us will link Rarity Inc to the jewels in a way we don't want to be linked. As for offering our services, there's no point. We've already verified the authenticity of the jewels."

"Do you have a better idea?" I scowled.

"Not at this moment."

I ran my hands through my hair. "If only Darcie hadn't moved those jewels before I arrived."

"Speaking of that woman." Marcus spoke cautiously. "Is she going to be at the auction tonight?"

"Not that I'm aware. I haven't invited her. In fact, she actually turned me down for lunch today."

"Good." His lips twitched. "We don't need her messing up our plans even more."

"Marcus."

"She has become a hindrance." He snipped.

"You should have predicted that when you met her at the Museum of Terra. She's involved because of you."

"She's involved because of you." Marcus countered furiously. "You leave tonight to me. Your head isn't in the game right now. Once we have Queen Mary's jewels, we're going home."

"Is this your subtle way of telling me to stop seeing her?"

"I don't care if you keep seeing her. I care that she may ruin the company's reputation by putting you behind bars."

I nodded. "I'll be more careful."

I had my meeting with Benoit today. He was just as nervous about having me in the building as he did the first time I was here earlier this week. Only this time, I'm not as pleasant. My failure last night affected my mood.

"Mr. Pinot." Benoit gestured to a seat. "What business do you need to discuss with me?"

"There have been rumours." I informed him.

"What kind of rumours?"

"Well, more like accusations." I corrected. "That someone has been stealing from the company."

Benoit swallowed hard. "I will conduct an extensive audit to find the culprit."

I held up a hand. "There's no need."

"Why not?"

"I already know it's you, Benoit."

"Me?" He flustered. "What makes you say that? I've been loyal to the company for years. So why would I need to steal from it?"

"I don't know the why, though I suspect it has something to do with your new wife." I told him flatly. "Marcus went over records and linked the missing money to you. I'm sorry, Benoit, but I have to let you go."

Benoit paled. "You can't. I need this job."

I shook my head. "Marcus and I have already found your replacement."

"But, Mr. Pinot."

I stood, going to the door. "You've been skimming off the top for the past two years. I do not tolerate thievery within my own company."

I know I sound like a hypocrite. Only Marcus would comment on it if he were here. I have to do this as CEO of Rarity Inc. Benoit stared at me. Letting him go was a difficult decision, but it had to be done. If I didn't do anything, others might think it was okay to steal from the company. I opened the door to let in the candidate Marcus, and I agreed upon.

"Frans will be your replacement." I told him. "I will give you two weeks to train him, and then I'm afraid you have to go, Benoit."

"Merci, Mr. Pinot." Frans shook my hand. "I will not waste this opportunity."

"If you need anything, please reach out. I expect great things. You're resume and work ethic are quite impressive."

With that, I left the office. I updated Benoit's secretary, who will now be Frans's secretary, on the management change. She didn't seem fazed by my decision to let Benoit go. Now that my business in France is complete, I can focus on the issue with Darcie.

The auction house was filled with rich-looking people dressed in floor-length dresses and suits. Marcus and I kept our eyes on the jewels as guests roamed the large room admiring everything up for auction before the event. Marcus said he has everything set up, but he's not telling me anything. I think he's afraid Darcie might get wind of our plans and ruin them again. However, I don't know how. *I wonder if she has me bugged.*

"What is she doing here?" Marcus' shocked tone revealed his annoyance.

I followed his gaze over to Darcie. *She's here?* "I have no idea, honest."

"Go find out. I don't want her interfering again."

I started toward her. Smiling as she saw me, she turned and walked away instead of returning the smile or meeting me halfway. *She ignored me!* Something was definitely going on in that mind of hers. She must know I'm Le Corbeau, or else she wouldn't be avoiding me — at least, I almost hope that's the case. I stopped to watch as she wandered over to Queen Mary's jewels. As if drawn to her, Jean Patrice sidled up next to her.

Get away from her! I wanted to storm up to them and pull Darcie away, but it might reveal my hand too much. So instead, I seethed as Jean Patrice's eyes roamed over her body and how he leaned in close to talk to her. The man is dangerous. He's known among criminals to get his hands dirty and do anything to make money — even destroy whatever he steals.

Thankfully, Josephine had him escorted out of the building. Josephine and Darcie talked briefly before they meandered out of sight. An announcement informed everyone that the auction was about to begin and urged guests to take seats. Marcus and I stood at the back of the auction room. Guests signed for numbered paddles before taking seats.

"Did you find out why she's here?" Marcus whispered.

"No." I shook my head. "She completely ignored me. But I did see her talking to Jean Patrice."

"That's good for us. She's diverted her attention his way." He frowned. "How did she even come across such a dangerous man?"

I wish I knew. I kept my eyes on Darcie, who kept her eyes on the guests. She lifted her wrist to her mouth. *She's security.* That explains why she's here. Josephine must have feared someone would steal the jewels after my failed attempt last night. Queen Mary's jewels came out next, and I shifted my attention to the guests. A woman in a black power suit stood off to the side, talking on the phone with a paddle in her free hand. Something about her seemed familiar. When

Queen Mary's jewels went to someone other than her, she turned to leave the room. That is when I saw her face.

"Impossible." My heart stopped, the word a mere whisper.

"What did you say?" Marcus whispered back.

"I saw her."

"Saw who?"

"Thea."

"Thea Stone?" He sounded worried. "You sure?"

"Positive."

"Well, shit. That's unexpected."

"I'm going after her."

"Don't." Marcus gripped my arm. "Your current woman is looking over here. If you follow Thea, it'll draw suspicion."

I looked toward the exit and then at Darcie. She was watching me. She then spoke into her wrist while watching me before slipping away backstage.

"I have to know why she's here."

I shook Marcus off and left the auction room. I paused to look down two hallways. One led to washrooms. The other led deeper into the building. I rushed down that hall only to have it split in two directions with no sign of Thea. I returned the way I came, making my way to the lobby. *Where did she go?*

I pushed the door to the outside and stepped out. Looking around, I tried to see any empty spaces in the parking lot from where her car could have been if she left already. Nothing. I don't know why I felt disappointed that I'd missed her. She nearly got me caught when she betrayed me. The rumble of an engine stopped my retreat inside. I turned back toward the parking lot just in time to see Thea drive past me as she floored it out of there. Three black SUVs followed after her shortly. I suspect it was Josephine's security. Returning to Marcus, he looked at me quizzically.

"She's gone." I shook my head.

"So is Darcie." He replied. "Since she left the room, she hasn't returned."

"That can't be good."

"Thea's presence here can't be good."

"She was probably after Queen Mary's jewels. Thea never could resist pretty things."

Marcus ran a hand through his hair. "This is getting too dangerous."

"I agree."

Chapter Eleven

♥

Darcie

I didn't expect to see Killian at the auction. *What is he doing here?* I couldn't afford to be distracted by him and actively avoided him. I'm working, and my focus must be on Queen Mary's jewels, not his blue eyes. Jean Patrice was another person I didn't expect to see at the auction. He looked at me like I was a stack of pancakes. He licked his lips and leaned in close when he talked. I jerked away from his touch. Josephine chose that moment to scold him for being there and had her larger, scarier, looking security men escort the man out.

When it was time for the auction to begin and the guests took seats, I moved to the stage. From there, I could watch everyone. I informed Tristan, who was backstage that the auction was starting. I paid extra attention to the guests when Queen Mary's jewels came up next to sell. Those who weren't bidding displayed only a slight interest in the jewels. It was those who were bidding that were most eager to possess the two pieces of jewellery. Finally, the auctioneer pronounced the jewels sold, and I watched a woman in a black power suit get up and leave the room. *She didn't look happy.*

Speaking in the mic at my wrist, I told Tristan about the woman in black. When he didn't answer, I tried calling him again. *Something's not right.* Worried, I went backstage to check on him. He wasn't there. I heard a scuffle just beyond where Queen Mary's jewels were sitting, waiting to be collected by their new owner. I inched closer. Someone in black was backing away from where I heard the skirmish sounds. The person turned to the jewels, and they stopped to stare upon seeing me. I registered bright red lips breaking out in a smile seconds before an electric bolt shot through me, knocking me unconscious.

When I arrived, the jewels were gone, and only a copycat of Le Corbeau's calling card remained. Police were beginning to arrive. I snagged the calling card — hopefully, before anyone noticed. Police questioned me. I told them I didn't see anything and lifted my shirt to show the marks left on my skin from the Taser used on me. After the police were done with me, I went to the security room. Tristan was talking to the police while holding an ice pack to his head.

"Are you okay?" I reached up to see if there was any damage and winced at the movement.

"I should ask you that."

"Taser."

He handed me the ice pack to put on my side.

"Thanks. What happened to you?"

"Knock out gas." He explained. "Hit my head on the desk on my way down."

"Can we go back to the hotel? I want to update Agent Moore."

He nodded his agreement. Before leaving, I checked in with Josephine. She wasn't mad about our failure to protect Queen Mary's jewels. She was more concerned for our safety. With Tristan's head injury, I got behind the wheel. The moment the hotel door closed, I put Agent Moore on speakerphone.

"Darcie, what can I do for you?" He greeted pleasantly.

"Kent, have you heard of a man named Jean Patrice?"

"I have. He's on the FBI watch list. But, unfortunately, any evidence collected against him has been circumstantial. Nothing has been concrete enough to prove his crimes. Why?"

"I've had a couple of run-ins with him."

"If he thinks you're a danger to him." He let the sentence drop.

I grimaced. "Right now, he's only been charming. However, I think he may have something to do with Paul's murder. He might also collaborate with the thief framing Le Corbeau."

"Any clues to indicate that?"

"A lot has happened." Tristan stated.

"Tell me everything." Agent Moore ordered.

I did, or rather we did. First, I told him about the link Marie found between Paul and Jean Patrice. Then, I told him about Jean Patrice showing up at the auction. Then, Tristan and I told Agent Moore what happened at the auction. Since we were in different areas and saw different things, it helped to complete the timeline of events. Agent Moore stayed silent as we explained everything.

"I will send agents to Paris to look into Jean Patrice. As for Le Corbeau, I traced his location to a hotel. However, it was not easy since he only briefly used the mirroring program."

My stomach lurched at the hotel name Agent Moore provided. *That's Killian's hotel.* Same blue eyes, same hotel, same feeling when kissed. I don't want to believe that Killian is Le Corbeau. I'd have to search his room for proof. Right now, it's not looking good. *I hope these two are not the same person.*

"What are we supposed to do with this information?" Tristan countered.

"Honestly, I don't think there's much else you can do without a badge." Agent Moore sighed. "Leave the rest to the FBI."

"Darcie, what are your thoughts?" Tristan asked me after we hung up.

"I'm not going home yet."

"What's the plan?"

"Sleep, I'm beat."

He laughed. "Good night Darcie."

Sleep did not come easily. I itched to confront Killian about the possibility of him being a thief. I also fear that he is a thief. *Don't get ahead of yourself, Darcie.* I tried to talk myself down, but images of Killian in an orange jumpsuit plagued me. If he is Le Corbeau, it proves how bad I am at picking a man for myself.

Tristan and I met Marie and Veronica for breakfast at Café Valentin. We talked about what happened at the auction house — only because Marie heard whispers, and Josephine called Veronica to check in on us. I then told Veronica that we'd be heading home very soon. She began to tear up but understood I couldn't stay in Paris forever. I told her to visit if things become too overwhelming in Paris. After paying their share, the two left Tristan and me to our coffees.

"What are we going to do about Le Corbeau?"

"Nothing." I answered, knowing this was something I was going to have to do myself. "I have a hunch, but I'd like to follow it up alone."

"Okay." He answered suspiciously. "What about Jean Patrice?"

"Agent Moore told us to leave him alone."

"But?"

"But if he's a loan shark, he should have records of his transactions with Paul."

He frowned. "He won't give you a copy even if you bat your eyes at him."

"I wasn't going to ask."

My attention was diverted to Killian, who had just walked into the café. After ignoring him at the auction, he sent me a tentative smile, unsure of my reaction. I returned the smile, which caused his to widen hopefully. Tristan turned to see who was there, and Killian's smile faltered. I couldn't help but laugh.

"Who is that?" Tristan inquired.

"The hot CEO." I used Veronica's description of him. A woman walked in and practically threw herself at him. *Who is she?* My stomach churned uneasily. "Let's go."

Tristan looked back again to see what I was seeing. Then, with a frown, he paid for our portion of the bill. Even if Killian did seem displeased with the woman, I had to remind myself that he was just a Paris fling. It's not like we agreed to have a relationship. *So why does it hurt so much to see him with another woman?* It could be someone he knows — like extended family or a friend. *Or a girlfriend.* Horrified with myself for sleeping with a man who may already be taken, I quickened my steps to the car.

"What do you want to do?"

"Tourist stuff." I answered and then looked at my phone as a text came in. "For a bit, anyway."

"Let me guess." He sighed while turning on the ignition. "You want to do surveillance on Jean Patrice's restaurant."

"And maybe find blueprints of the building too."

"Le Corbeau has rubbed off on you." Tristan teased. "Are you sure you'll be able to find any evidence in the restaurant?"

I shrugged. "I have to try Tristan."

"I know, Darcie, but this is dangerous."

"Which is why I'm not asking you to help. There's no reason for us to get caught. The boss would kill us."

"The boss would kill me if I let you do this alone. So I'll think of some way to keep Jean Patrice occupied. He hasn't met me yet, so he won't be as suspicious."

Killian: I think there was a misunderstanding.

I stared at the text Killian sent me after Tristan, and I drove away from the café. I've been debating with myself all morning on whether or not I should respond. I need answers. Determined, I replied to Killian — eventually.

Me: What misunderstanding?

Killian: The woman who threw herself onto me is an ex from six years ago.

Me: So?

Killian: So, I want you to know I have no feelings for her. Except for hatred.

Me: She obviously still has feelings for you.

Killian: I don't care if she does. I care if you do.

My breath hitched. That's some statement for someone who has only known me for a few days.

Killian: Let me show you tomorrow.

Me: Show me what?

Killian: How much I care for you. I have some business to attend to tonight. Tomorrow I can be all yours before I fly home the next day.

I bit my bottom lip. This could be my chance to prove whether Killian is or is not Le Corbeau.

Me: Fine. I'll text you when I'm on my way to the hotel tomorrow.

Chapter Twelve

Le Corbeau

"Killian!" Thea threw herself onto me.

I shoved her off, but Darcie had already left Café Valentin by the time I did. "What do you want, Thea?"

"It's been so long."

"Six years."

"See? So long." She purred.

"Not long enough." I growled.

Exiting the café, I watched Darcie drive by. *She ruined my chance with Darcie.* I had hoped her smile meant she was willing to talk. We needed to talk. I want to know if I did anything to upset her, and I wanted to apologize for it. I also wanted to know who the man was that she was with.

"You stole the Crystal Owl from me, leaving me to get caught by the cops."

Thea frowned, eyes on the same car I was watching. "That was so long ago. You need to let the past go, Killian."

"What do you want, Thea?"

"A trade."

I began my trek back to the hotel. Thea, unfortunately, followed. The woman is persistent. She's also more beautiful than I remember, taller and more confident. I held onto my anger, refusing to fall victim to the charm that had once enraptured me.

"I'm not interested in anything you have to say."

"I missed you, Killian." She pouted.

That pout used to work on me. I'd give her anything when she pouted. *Won't work now.* I clenched my hands into fists and kept walking. I don't even want to look at her, fear that I might give in to the old feelings she had once stirred inside me.

"I didn't." I stated coldly. "Tell me about this trade so I can get rid of you."

"The Eye for Queen Mary's jewels." Her flirtatious tone was replaced with a business-like manner. "Of course, if you don't want them, I'll hand them off to my employer."

"And who is your employer?"

She just smiled. "Someone who would appreciate The Eye more than Queen Mary's jewels."

I stopped walking. If I can get those jewels and even the Purple Onyx, then maybe I can get back into Darcie's good graces. Having so many gems in my possession at once would be risky. She knows I don't have the jewels, but she'd probably be pleased if they were all returned. Thankful even. *I wonder if I could gain a kiss as a reward.*

"Purple Onyx." I countered, stopping to look at her.

"I don't have it."

"Who does?"

She leaned in to whisper the answer. "Jean Patrice."

Of course, he does. "Fine. The Eye for Queen Mary's jewels."

"Excellent! I'll contact you later to set up the trade."

I won't let her have The Eye. Seemingly satisfied, she kissed my cheek — which I wiped off — and left me on the streets of Paris. I continued my walk back to the hotel. So much for leaving Paris this afternoon. First, I called the airport to change my flight to catch one for the late afternoon the following day.

Marcus wasn't too impressed with my decision to stay when he came knocking on my door — which reminded me to extend my stay at this hotel. He was even less impressed with Thea's trade offer. I asked him to prepare a fake Eye to hand over to her. When I return home, I'll return the real Eye to its owner. He left for the airport with parting words: clean up this mess. *Don't have to tell me twice.*

Darcie eventually texted me. Reading between the lines, she sounded pissed, or maybe that was hurt that she conveyed in her words. I convinced her to have another date with me before I left. Something told me I wouldn't see her again once we left Paris. Now that I know where to find the Purple Onyx, I need to steal that tonight. No way am I letting Jean Patrice keep something so precious. Who knows what he'll do with it.

I parked a block away from Jean Patrice's Chinese restaurant and then used the back alleys to reach my destination. I need to get that gem. The Purple Onyx will be here based on the last time I stole from him at his Canadian-based restaurant.

I made my way up the metal stairs to the backdoor on the second level. With a flashlight in my mouth, I pulled lock picks out of my back pocket and started my work. *I hate lock-picking.* I'm better with a safe — both dial and electric. Focused on the lock, I did not hear anyone come up the metal stairs.

"You going to unlock that?"

The sudden voice had me jumping back and falling down a step on my ass as I stared up in surprise. "Kitten?"

"I'm not going to ask you why you're here." She knelt, picked up the lock picks I dropped, and unlocked the door in seconds.

"I think I just fell even more in love with you."

She frowned, handing the tools back. "I'm on a clock."

"What are you even doing here?" I stood brushing off. "Breaking into a building, isn't that against your code?"

Her frown deepened. "None of your business."

"You know, I love this side of you."

Darcie looked away and slipped into the building without a word. I'm unsure what was going through her mind, but I'm intrigued. Following, I became her shadow as she maneuvered to Jean Patrice's office without pause. *She knows the way.* Either she's been here before, which doesn't sit well with me, or she's studied the layout. Picking locks and learning floor plans, this side of my little Kitten is sexy. I can't wait to see what other surprises she has for me.

"What are you looking for?" I questioned after closing the door to the office.

"What are you here to steal?" She countered, searching the desk with gloved hands and the flashlight on her phone.

"I asked first."

Darcie didn't answer me right away. "Evidence."

Intriguing. "What kind of evidence?"

"You didn't answer my question."

"I got a tip. All I'm doing is checking its authenticity." I ignored the safe on the floor, which probably held money for the restaurant. Instead, I ran my fingers along the edge of an ornate frame on the opposite wall. A subtle click and it swung right open. "Bingo."

"What did you find?" Darcie looked up and then came over to see.

"A safe."

"Can you get it open?"

"For a kiss." I grinned at her.

"Now is not the time for jokes."

"Who said I'm joking?"

"Are you just trying to buy time?" She taunted. "Because you can't unlock it just like the back door?"

"When I unlock this safe, I expect a kiss."

Nothing. Wait. Was that a shadow of a smile? The last time I broke into Jean Patrice's safe, he used his grandfather's birthday. With luck, he's used the same code. Yep. The door swung open. Darcie held up her flashlight. We could see loose papers, a tattered book — make that three tattered books and a black pouch. I grabbed the pouch, peeking inside.

"Is that what you came for?" She reached in and pulled out a book.

"Apparently. Did you find your evidence?"

She closed the book she was flipping through. "I hope so."

"Now, about that kiss."

"No time." She looked at her phone. "We have to go."

I closed the safe, following her out. Unfortunately, we only made it halfway to our exit when footsteps could be heard approaching. I pulled Darcie into a random room — a storage room, based on the legal boxes and supplies surrounding us. We kept an ear to the door. The footsteps thankfully kept going before we slipped out and made our escape.

"That was fun." I grinned at her.

"Fun is not the word I would use."

"Come on, Dar — uh, Kitten." I caught myself about to say her name.

"Dar?"

Unfortunately, she caught it. I winced. Thinking fast, I came up with a plausible excuse.

"Darling Kitten. But I don't think that suits you."

Darcie narrowed her eyes at me as I started backing away. "Forget something?"

"Did I?"

"You did." She looked down at her phone. "Got to go."

Just then, I remembered the kiss I asked for. Grabbing her arm, I pulled her to me. Her lips were soft against mine. She didn't fight me and let me kiss her, but she didn't lean in for more.

"Good night Kitten."

Chapter Thirteen

Darcie

I stayed up with Tristan for hours, reviewing the book and researching every name. It is a ledger, a page per person, indicating how much money was borrowed from the loan shark. I might have quickly flipped through the book before running away with it, but I wasn't sure it contained Paul's name. Thankfully, it did. Even with the diagonal red line across the page, his name could still be read at the top. A few other names in the book were marked the same way, and with some research, we found out those people were also killed.

I woke up the following day with Tristan. His arm slung loosely around me as I slept on his chest. I don't even remember going to sleep. I pushed away from my partner, taking over the shower first. Coming out, I found Tristan gone. He returned shortly with a white box topped with a red bow.

"What is that?"

"Front desk called while you were in the shower." He put it on the bed before going to his bag to grab some clothes. "They said this was dropped off for you early this morning."

"Did they see who delivered it?" I eyed the box suspiciously.

"Nope. It was just sitting on the reception desk with your name on the tag."

"Did you look inside?"

"A glance." Tristan announced before closing the bathroom door.

I sat on the bed and moved the white box to my lap. The tag had my name written neatly on its surface. Very carefully, I opened the lid to peek inside. A folded piece of paper was tucked next to a black pouch. Pulling out the note, I read the message: It was fun working with you last night. Hope this helps, Kitten. Setting the note next to me, I pulled out the black pouch and dumped its contents into my hand.

Tristan exited the bathroom, stopped beside me, and frowned at the Purple Onyx I held. He reached for the note, and his frown deepened. He started talking, but I wasn't listening. *How did Le Corbeau know where I was staying?* I suspected he must have followed me from the restaurant. I replaced the jewel within the pouch with a frown and looked at the tag again: Darcie Manners. *Dar, was he about to call me Darcie?* Yet again, I couldn't help but wonder if Killian and Le Corbeau are the same person. I don't recall ever telling the thief my name.

Tristan's flight is scheduled for today. I took him to the airport, promised him I won't miss my flight back home tomorrow then returned to the hotel. Tonight, I have plans with Killian. Tonight, I'll figure out if he's Le Corbeau. I packed my suitcase and checked out, no longer needing my hotel room. Before going to Killian, I needed to stop at the police station. Detective Giome will be interested in both the book and the jewel.

There was a strange tension within the police station among the officers. When Jean Patrice came out of the captain's office, I understood why. Not wanting him to see me, I maneuvered to hide behind an officer, tucking the book behind my back and into the waistband of my jeans. He scanned the room and stormed straight for Marie. She was coming out of a hall with files in her arms. Jean Patrice blocked her path and glared down at her. She reminded me of a scared bunny. Marie gripped the files tighter, her shoulders hunched in as she shrank away from him.

"Vous m'avez volé." His voice was loud enough for everyone to hear.

"Je ne l'ai pas fait." Marie's voice was thin, her fear of him evident. "Je ne sais pas de quoi vous parlez."

"Don't lie to me."

I quickly set the white box on Detective Giome's desk and rushed to Marie's rescue. No one else seemed to make a move to help. I pulled my shirt lower in the back to verify that the evidence of the book was covered.

"You've been to my restaurant twice this week." Jean Patrice accused. "Then, last night, I was robbed."

"She's not lying." I inserted myself into the conversation.

Jean Patrice smiled tightly. "Come to save your police friend?"

"She was with me last night."

"Liar."

I smiled tightly. "Would you rather hear that Le Corbeau stole from you last night?"

Jean Patrice frowned. "How do you know that name?"

"I know a lot more than that name." I threatened, voice lowering. "More than you're willing to admit in front of cops that don't have your money lining their pockets."

He stared at me, deciding his next move. Then he smiled. "You should work for me."

"Not going to happen." I shook my head. "Now, leave Marie alone. If I hear that you've been harassing her in any way, I'll ensure that what I know gets to the proper authorities."

"Be careful whom you threaten, ma belle." Jean Patrice warned. "I have friends everywhere."

We glared at each other, neither of us backing down. Finally, the captain's office door opened, and he ordered everyone to return to work. Jean Patrice took that as his cue to leave the station. Marie visibly shook in her healed boots. I took her in my arms and helped her to her desk.

"Marie." Detective Giome rushed over, crouching to be at eye level with her. "Tu vas bien?"

Marie looked over at me. "How are you so brave, Darcie?"

"I'm not." I admitted, leaning forward in the chair I'd slumped into next to her desk. "I'm stupid."

"I don't understand."

"I just lied to and threatened a dangerous criminal."

A laugh bubbled up out of her. "You are stupid."

"What's this about threatening Jean Patrice?" Detective Giome glared at me.

"Nicolas." Marie soothed. "Elle m'a sauvé."

He took a moment to watch Marie before turning to me. "Merci."

"You're welcome." I smiled at him. "I have more. On your desk is a gift. It was delivered to my hotel this morning, but it'll be more useful in your hands." I pulled the book out from behind my back. "This book proves that Paul and many others have been using a loan shark. Marie can prove that Paul has been going from Jean Patrice's Chinese restaurant and a casino."

"How did you get this?" Detective Giome narrowed his eyes on me.

"It is better you don't know."

He took it reluctantly. "I won't be able to use this."

"Maybe not." I shrugged, standing. "But it could be a useful lead."

I hugged Marie, thanking her for being there for Veronica. I tried to contact my best friend for a final goodbye, but the call went to voicemail. So the only thing I can do now is contact Killian. The man waited for me in the lobby. He offered to go out for lunch, but I suggested room service. I need time to figure out if he's Le Corbeau and how I feel about that — and him. Killian had no complaint about taking me to his room. He wrapped an arm around my waist, tucking me into his side and guided me to the elevator.

Over lunch, on the terrace, we talked. *He is really easy to talk to.* I told him about Veronica and her loss — leaving critical pieces of information out as technically, the case is still open. Still, I feel like my responsibility to my best friend on this matter is done. He sat there listening like every word out of my mouth was more important than his next breath. I asked about his business here with Rarity Inc., and he said it's concluded and that he's already promoted someone to replace the person he's had to let go.

"I'm delighted you're here, Darcie." We migrated inside to the couch as a breeze began to pick up. "I thought you were mad at me."

"Not mad, just needing space. You took up a lot of mental space that I needed."

"And now?" He brushed his fingers along my cheek.

I leaned into him. *There's no way he's a thief. He can't be.* "You and only you."

Killian brushed my lips tentatively. The thrill that went through me was arousing. I leaned into him, shifting to straddle his lap. Killian wrapped me in his arms, pressing me into him. The feel of his arms around me brought a sense of protection. His kiss made me feel loved. *Loved.* That thought made me pause. *I must be mistaken. I can't love a Paris fling, can I?*

"Are you okay?" Killian questioned. There was genuine concern in his tone.

I cupped his face, a forced smile on my lips. "Just fine."

He smiled back, hands rubbing my back soothingly. I kissed him again. In just a few short days, Killian Pinot crashed through every barrier I made after Phillip's betrayal. I lost myself in this man. We stopped to order room service for supper before all the attention returned to pleasure.

At some point, we made it to the bedroom, where hands and mouths did quite a bit of exploring. Killian lifted the top of his suitcase, pulling out a box of condoms, and I swear I saw Le Corbeau's mask within. Dred started to set in — until his lips touched my skin. The feel of Killian buried deep inside, his movements loving — ensuring I felt every inch of pleasure. *Mind-blowing.* I lost track of how many orgasms he pulled out of me.

I woke sometime in the night with Killian's arm around my waist, holding me against him. Warmth filled me, along with a need to go pee. Slipping out from under the sheets, I went to relieve my bladder. Returning to the bedroom, my eyes drifted over to the suitcase. I really shouldn't have, but I did anyway. With no light, I had to trust my sense of touch as I felt around in the suitcase. My heart dropped as it touched something hard, and upon further inspection realized it was a mask. *Le Corbeau's mask.*

I dropped it, got dressed and ran out of the hotel. Killian Pinot, CEO of Rarity Inc., is also Le Corbeau, a thief. My heart broke. I felt betrayed and played for a fool. Unfortunately, I was right: I have a terrible judgment of boyfriends. No more dating for me, the men I keep choosing hurt me.

Chapter Fourteen

Le Corbeau

When I woke up, Darcie was gone — just like last time. I had hoped she would stay for breakfast this time before my flight. To make sure, I checked both the terrace and living room. She was gone. Then, snatching my phone from where I left it in the living room, I texted her.

Me: Morning, beautiful.

I waited for a response. When I received none, I texted her again.

Me: I wanted to have breakfast together before I caught my flight.

Nothing. I couldn't have been that bad of a lover. I made sure she was pleasured, and she seemed to enjoy every inch of it. Then, returning to the bedroom, I went for a shower. In need of fresh clothes, I flipped open the suitcase and found Le Corbeau's mask on top of everything. *Fuck!* If Darcie found that, then it could be the reason she left so early. Or maybe she didn't want to say goodbye since we never did talk about continuing to see each other after Paris. I doubt that was the reason for her departure.

Unfortunately, I don't have time to find out — I have a plane to catch. The ten-hour flight home was agonizing. I couldn't get Darcie, or the fear that she saw the mask, out of my head. I'm unsure if I should prepare for her to storm Rarity Inc. with an arrest warrant or if I have time to convince her not to arrest me.

Me: I just got back home. I hope you had a good flight for your return.

Still nothing.

I should warn Marcus. First, I need to return The Eye to its owner. Marcus should have the fake Eye ready by now. Thea will likely contact me soon for the trade. There is no way I'm giving her the authentic Eye. As for Queen Mary's jewels, I'll send them back to Josephine once they are in my possession.

Marcus didn't react the way I thought he would when I told him that Darcie might know I'm Le Corbeau. Instead, he asked me how I was. *How am I?* That's a good question. I haven't entirely processed everything. How will I be if she knows the truth? Relieved? Heartbroken? I fell for her, and I fell hard. Maybe I'm cursed when it comes to women in my life.

Marcus helped me plan the return of The Eye. This helped to keep my mind off Darcie. That is until she finally texted me a week later, after all my pestering.

Darcie: I don't want to see you anymore.

I stared at the message.

Me: That's a shame because I want to see you.

Darcie: And don't text me either. I want nothing to do with you, Killian Pinot. The fling we had in Paris was a mistake. Or maybe it was all part of some plan, Le Corbeau.

My heart sank.

Me: You were never some plan. You were a pleasant surprise in my life. A precious jewel I wish to keep.

Darcie: I won't arrest you right away, thief. But know that when I do come to slap the cuffs on your wrists, you won't be able to weasel yourself out of them this time.

Heartbroken. I feel heartbroken. She knows the truth, and our time together meant nothing. Losing her hurts even more than Thea's betrayal.

Chapter Fifteen

♥

Darcie

Despite leaving Killian in Paris, disappearing during the night, and even changing my flight last minute to return home much sooner — he still texted me. *The nerve of him, talking like he didn't lie to me.* I had to change his personalized text sound to silent. Hearing the ping of a new message coming from him hurt too much. I tried to ignore him. It didn't work. Killian wouldn't stop attempting to reach out. *I have to make things clear.* I told him I wanted nothing to do with him. His response sounded confused, and he tried to assure me with sweet words that he didn't want our time in Paris to be just a fling. *I won't fall for it.*

I informed Agent Moore about Le Corbeau's true identity — a week after returning from Paris. He had the audacity to tell me we couldn't go out immediately to arrest him, something about not having enough proof. But arresting the thief will be the only way to get him to stop texting me. Before storming off, I said some things I probably shouldn't have to Agent Moore. My battered heart can't take much more of

Killian's attempts to apologize and explain. Now that I know the truth, a truth that he is admitting to, I'm being told there's not enough evidence to arrest the thief, even after working so hard to prove that Le Corbeau exists in the first place.

Holst Security gun range is where I found myself. Shooting my anger, frustration, and hurt away. I think I went through three magazines before Agent Moore found me. Startled, I aimed the gun at him. I blinked back the wetness in my eyes as I lowered the weapon, emptied the chamber, and placed it on the table.

"Kent, don't sneak up on me like that." I chastised, trying to cover my embarrassment of pointing the gun at him.

"Your partner told me what happened in Paris."

"What exactly did Tristan tell you?" New anger boiled inside.

"That you fell for Killian Pinot and that he felt bad for telling you to keep seeing him." He smiled softly. "If you knew he was Le Corbeau from the start, you would have dealt with it differently."

"How do you know that?"

He stepped closer. "Because you were determined to put a criminal behind bars. As I said earlier, there is no proof that Killian Pinot is Le Corbeau."

"What do you need?"

"A confession would be nice."

"He's confessed to me over text."

Agent Moore shook his head. "He'd need to confess to law enforcement. But, unfortunately, even a confession without physical evidence won't hold up well in court."

"I can get that."

"No." Agent Moore's tone hardened as he stared down at me. "You cannot be near this case anymore. Your emotions will skew the evidence."

I wanted to scream at him that he was wrong, but that's just the kind of emotion he was referring to. "Then what can I do, Kent?"

"Trust me, Darcie." He brushed some hair behind my ear. "I will put this criminal in jail for you. It may take some time, but I will see you smile again."

With that final note, he left me. *What the hell does that mean?* I looked back at the gun on the table. I'd lost the energy to shoot any more paper targets. After cleaning everything up, I went back upstairs. The boss gave Tristan and me a simple job: security at an environmental conference. The event planners have received threats regarding some of their speakers and are nervous they might be acted upon. *This is what I need. Work.* A distraction from the turmoil within.

Agent Moore returned to the FBI with a promise to keep in touch while Tristan and I returned to our routine. The boss seemed to sense that I needed to stay busy so my mind wouldn't wander. Something I was very grateful for. At night, when I'm all alone, I miss Killian's touch.

Two months later, Agent Moore returned with a small team of fellow FBI agents.

"Agent Moore, what are you doing here?" Tristan questioned.

"Local police asked us to help with a drug case." He replied, smiling at me. "Do you mind if I talk to the two of you?"

"Is this about Le Corbeau?" I asked hopefully.

He shook his head and led us to the boss' office. My hope shattered. Agent Moore hadn't sent me any updates on the Le Corbeau case. I itched to know what he was doing and how soon it would be before the thief was arrested.

The boss didn't look surprised to see his friend. "I heard you were back in town."

"And I heard you are involved in my case."

The boss grinned. "Darcie, Tristan, it looks like you'll be collaborating with Agent Moore again."

"I don't understand." I admitted.

"Yesterday, Mr. Johnson signed a contract wanting us to protect his daughter by looking into her boyfriend. We will do this covertly as his relationship with her is rocky."

"How does this relate to Agent Moore's case?" Tristan countered.

"Women have been showing up naked and murdered with signs of possible rape." Agent Moore explained. "Toxicology reports all state that there was also a drug in their system known as Blue Devil. Along with some other new cocktail that appears to change slightly with each victim as if they are guinea pigs."

"That's horrible." I took a seat, feeling my stomach turn at the news. "I'm still not seeing the connection, though."

"Blue Devil comes from a drug dealer named Scott Flowers. FBI has been watching him for the past couple of years. His network around the world is impressive. We've removed a few men on the bottom of the totem, but no one will give Flowers up. This is also the first-time murder has been linked to his pills."

"Scott Flowers." Boss cut in before I could repeat the question. "Is the boyfriend we are to be looking into."

Now the pieces fit. "Okay. We know the boyfriend is bad for Miss Johnson. So, let's tell the client so he can pull his daughter away from him."

"Here's the thing." Agent Moore supplied. "Even if you get Miss Johnson out, Flowers will find another girl. So I want your help to shut him down completely."

"You are not going to use Darcie as bait." Tristan shook his head. "It is too dangerous."

"All she needs to do is get in, get a recording of Flowers dealing drugs, then get out. FBI will work with local narcotics to finalize the details."

"I still don't like it. What if he doesn't hand her any drugs?"

"Then we'll figure something else out."

"No."

"I'll do it." I cut in.

Tristan glared at me, but Agent Moore smiled proudly.

"Excellent. Flowers owns a club downtown. Local law enforcement has been able to integrate one of their own as a bouncer into the club. He'll let you right in. Once inside, you'll be on your own, but I'll ensure you're wired so we can get you out if anything goes sideways."

"When?"

"Tonight."

"Then I better get home and change."

"I'll pick you up and drive you to the club."

"I'll drive her." Tristan interjected.

Agent Moore nodded. "Then come with me. I'll give you what you need to get her wired. Darcie?"

"Yes?"

"Do be careful tonight."

The things we do for our clients. I returned home to shower, get dressed and style my hair. To catch a drug dealer's eye, I needed to look my best: short dress, high heels, perfectly wavy hair, and subtle makeup. Makeup took the longest. I even had to pull up videos on perfecting the smoky eye. In a few short hours, Tristan came to pick me up.

A low whistle passed his lips. "You're looking extra hot."

"Thank you." I laughed lightly.

"If you can't grab Scott Flowers' eye in that dress, the FBI will never get the man."

"I hope they do." I bit my lip, nerves starting to take over. "Scott Flowers sounds dangerous."

"FBI made you some special earrings. We'll be listening to everything. If anything goes south, I'll come running. There's even a necklace with a hidden camera."

"Real spy pieces."

I locked up behind me and followed him out to his car. The electronic jewellery he spoke of was found in the glove box. Nerves were beginning to take hold.

"You don't have to do this." Tristan stated softly as he started the car.

"Too late for that."

"Agent Moore could have sent an FBI agent in. You didn't have to agree to be the bait."

"This involves our client. If we don't help get Scott Flowers off the streets, he could go after Miss Johnson again. We are assigned to protect her."

Tristan scowled. "I don't like you going in. Especially since you're still hurting."

I twisted in the seat, turning away. "I'm fine."

"Darcie."

"I'm fine." I bit out.

Tristan sighed reluctantly. "Let's go over the plan tonight."

"Catch the eye of Scott Flowers, then catch him on tape — both video and sound selling drugs. I'm in, then out."

"Good, and remember, I'll hear and see what's going on, but I'll have no way to communicate with you."

"I know."

Tristan dropped me off a block away from the club. Nerves made my legs wobbly as I slid out of the car. *You can do this, Darcie.* Scott Flowers has killed women, and I won't be another victim. I'm to provide evidence of his drug dealing ways. I'm to help put a criminal away in jail. Scott Flowers won't slip away from law enforcement like Le Corbeau.

The placed bouncer let me in with a simple nod of his head. The dance club was packed. The music was at the perfect level — just loud enough for the base to vibrate through the frame, but still able to have a conversation without yelling too loudly. Bodies writhed on the dance floor to the beat, sensual and provocative. It would look like a giant orgy if no one wore any clothes. I cringed at the mental image.

I did a quick sweep of the club for the criminal. *Not on the dance floor or at the bar.* Scott Flowers couldn't be seen on the upper level. However, as I moved further into the club, I barely saw him in a booth on the main floor. I shot him a flirtatious look before sliding into a stool at the bar strategically in his line of sight. Ordering a vodka soda, I sat there babying the drink and shooting glances toward Scott Flowers, wondering what my next move would be.

"You need to talk to Killian."

I turned in the stool to stare dumbfounded at Marcus. *What is he doing here?* I had to think fast. He'll only ruin this operation. And this conversation isn't something I want to be recorded for Tristan and the FBI to hear.

"Leave me alone." I slid off the bar stool with my drink. "Now is not a good time."

"Not a good time?" He laughed bitterly, following me. "Killian is a wreck."

Really? My heart tightened at the news. *Why am I happy to hear that?* Marcus grabbed my arm, forcing me to look at him.

"Let me go." I pulled my arm away, tone high pitched. Then without thinking, I threw my drink at him. "Stay away from me!"

Scott Flowers slid up next to me. "I think it's time for you to leave."

Marcus glared. "I was right about you."

Security had snuck up, waiting to escort him out. I felt terrible about what I did, but it had to be done. I didn't expect the situation to turn in my favour and bring Scott Flowers to me.

Scott turned to me. "Are you okay?"

I nodded. "A little shaken."

"Maybe I can help."

"Really? How?" I tried to sound hopeful with a touch of intrigue in my tone.

A slow smile graced his face. He offered me his hand. I hesitated just enough. Scott led me upstairs. First names were exchanged as he walked us past more booths with clubgoers, then down a quiet hall and opened a restricted door. I hoped this was getting recorded because fear laced itself into my gut.

"Have a seat." He gestured to the only available spot in the room. "I'll get you a water."

I sat right on the edge of a bed. I haven't caught any evidence against Scott Flowers, but this situation made me very uncomfortable. He went behind a bar returning with a bottle of water and a blue pill. Little horns and a devil's tail are printed on the round pill. Blue Devil, I assumed. Scott Flowers told me it's a muscle relaxer, then watched as I placed it in my mouth, took a swig of water, then swallowed. Then, with a smile, he took the bottle from me, turning his back. In that instant, I pulled the pill out from under my tongue and tucked it quickly into my bra before he turned around.

When he did turn back to me, his lips found mine. *Gross!* I scooted back on the bed. Unfortunately, he followed. His knee wedged itself between my legs. I stopped crawling to push him back. *Useless.* A prick in my neck was the only warning of more drugs being forced into me before my vision blurred to darkness.

I woke with a groan. My neck and shoulders were sore, and my eyelids were heavy. It took a while for my brain to catch up. When it did, I bolted upright, taking stock of my surroundings. I was in a different room — a larger room with a bar, pool table, and lots of chairs. Scott Flowers sat in one of those comfy-looking chairs, his dress shirt open, his belt undone, and a drink in his hand as he watched me.

"About time you woke up."

"How long was I out?" I scooted away from him, still sitting on a bed. "Where am I?"

"Only a couple of hours. Do you realize how tempting you are?"

A couple of hours? Where's Tristan? I swallowed past the fear that rose quickly.

"This isn't the club."

"Yes and no." He answered vaguely. "It's not the club you entered, but it is a club."

I reached for the necklace, the sound of metal drawing my eyes to my hand. Wide cuffs covered my wrists, hooked to a chain that disappeared behind a mountain of pillows at the head of the bed. Grabbing hold of the chain, I tugged. Not surprised that I couldn't pull free, but I knew that. I tugged to see how much length I had. Not much, maybe a couple of feet. I'm pretty much confined to the bed.

"You're mine." His sickening statement drew my attention back to Scott, and he grinned. "I was warned about

130

you. A business friend said to be weary of a brown-haired, hazel-eyed woman named Darcie."

"Who told you?"

"Jean Patrice. You riled him up. It makes me even more excited to have you."

He must have taken my threat very seriously. "That won't happen. I have friends who will be worried about me and come looking."

"I'm well aware the FBI have been sniffing around so that necklace you were reaching for was left in the club for them to find. As for finding you, that won't be for a few days. When I'm done having my fun with you."

"You will be arrested. That necklace you left behind was recording, and it would have caught you handing me a Blue Devil."

"I'm not worried." He picked up a small bag of yellow pills from a small table beside his chair. "You're going to help me test the new batch of Sunshine."

"I don't think so."

"Not willingly, of course. The first few batches didn't work out, so I hope this batch will succeed."

I stared at the bag, preparing to fight back, even if all I had were my legs free. "What is Sunshine supposed to do?"

Scott moved closer, placing his drink and bag on a side table beside the bed. I waited for him to get on the bed before kicking out. Unfortunately, he seemed to anticipate the move and caught my legs. Pulling me closer, the dress rose to my waist before he straddled me. I could have gotten him off me if my wrists weren't chained above my head, restricting my movements. Instead, all I could do was squirm, his weight on my stomach stopping me from squirming out from under him.

Scott reached for the glass and bag, ensuring he didn't shift his weight too much or else I'd have a chance to get away. He took a swig of his drink and then forced a pill into my mouth. Before I could spit it out, he covered my mouth with his. The beverage tasted like straight vodka. I couldn't hold it for long, and I had to swallow.

Pulling back, Scott caressed my cheek. "It shouldn't take long now."

"What do you expect to happen?" The vodka burned, making my voice sound raspy.

"There's a lot of science involved, but to put it bluntly, darling, you're going to have a strong need for sex. A pleasure I'm going to provide happily, and you will enjoy every minute of it. I'm told Sunshine will increase the intensity of the orgasm."

"So, you created a rape drug?" My heartbeat picked up, and I started to feel weird. *Tristan! Agent Moore!*

"Is it rape when the woman begs for sexual release?"

"You drugged the other women — drugged me — forcing that unwilling confession."

"Unwilling confession?" Scott smiled. His lips were on mine in a soft kiss as his hands massaged my breasts through the dress's fabric. "Tell me what you're feeling, Darcie."

That damned drug is messing with my brain. His touch felt good, and I almost moaned when he sucked on my collarbone. I fought hard against the effects of the drug.

"Free my hands. I'll show you what I'm feeling."

Scot stared at me, assessing. "I quite like you chained up."

Shit. I had hoped that a flirtatious line would work while I could still think rationally. Scott crawled off me, his head ducking between my legs to kiss my inner knee, slowly moving further up. *Hell no!* Panic seemed to override the drug. I kicked him in the face and scrambled as far away from him as possible.

He growled, holding his nose. "I think you need another dose."

He lunged at me, taking another pill from the bag and pinning me to the headboard despite my attempts to keep him at bay with my feet. Another yellow pill was forced into my mouth, with his hand over my mouth and his thumb and finger pinching my nose. I couldn't breathe. Right when I thought I would suffocate, he let me go. Taking in a deep breath, I also took in the pill. A second dose of Sunshine went down my throat. *This can't be good.*

I choked on the dry pill. "Bastard!"

Scott got off the bed and removed his shirt and pants before returning, thankfully still in his briefs. The second dose of that drug hit me hard. My muscles relaxed, and my skin felt extra sensitive. Proof of that was the shiver that ran over me from the gentle finger he ran up my leg.

"This is going to be fun."

Crawling back on the bed, Scott wrapped my legs around his waist. I could feel his hard length against me. Then, holding my hips, he ground against me. A groan slipped past my lips.

"You want this?" He growled.

I forced my head from side to side. My stomach curdled with fear.

"I know you do." He ground into me again. "You'll beg for it. Then I'll fuck you so hard that you won't need Sunshine to beg for my cock."

He leaned down to capture my lips. His hand gripped my breast hard. Resistance to the drug was futile. The double dose of Sunshine was against me. My body unwillingly arched into him.

Scott smiled. "This dress has got to go."

"Don't." I forced out.

"You're right. It'll take too much time."

Fear couldn't pierce through the haze of the Sunshine drug this time. My muscles were relaxed, yet my core tightened with a need for a release. Scott hovered over me, watching me.

"Tell me what you need, Darcie. Tell me you need my cock."

Somewhere in the distance, I heard a crash and sounds that might have been a sign of my rescue. However, I did feel Scott pull away from me.

"Darcie." Tristan's voice called to me. "I'll get you free."

"Sunshine." I mumbled, not sure if I was coherent. "New drug."

"What?"

I'm unsure what happened, but I moaned as his arms lifted me.

"You're safe now, Darcie. I've got you."

Chapter Sixteen

Le Corbeau

I tried reaching out, but Darcie still ignored me. She wouldn't even let me explain. I don't blame her — I tricked and lied to her. No sane woman would want anything to do with me. I deserve the cold shoulder, but I can't get her out of my mind. Even Thea's visit to exchange Queen Mary's jewels for the fake Eye didn't faze me. I could return all the treasures that I've stolen, which I planned to anyway, but it won't bring Darcie back to me.

I fell hard. She stole my heart. I was supposed to steal her heart. The depression of not having her by my side or even being able to talk to her got to me. I stopped going to work, unable to fully concentrate. Marcus agreed that taking time off was a good idea, knowing how I reacted after Thea.

I couldn't help but replay every moment we had together. In those memories, I wondered if there was any way to avoid this outcome. If she had never met me, could we have continued as Le Corbeau and Kitten? What would have happened if I met her first? How long could I have kept the two lives separate? Could I have been more careful? If I had more time, would Darcie have come to love both sides of me?

That line of thinking sent me spiralling even further. I'm unsure how long I stayed in my house before Marcus stopped by. He looked at me disgusted. He cleaned the dishes and take-out containers I'd begun to neglect, then ordered me to shower. The water didn't help my mood. I just returned to the couch. With an irritated sigh, Marcus made me an offer: he'll check in on Darcie. If she's moved on, I need to move on, but if she's broken, I have to man up and talk to her. It sounded reasonable. I secretly wished she was hurt.

Two days later, Marcus returned. "She's moved on."

"She's happy without me?"

"I found her at a club. When I tried to talk to her, she yelled at me and threw her drink at me. Then some guy came up next to her — her knight in shining armour and had me kicked out."

Anger and hurt flooded my system. I turned the TV on, not wanting to think about Darcie in the arms of another man. A news anchor was standing outside a club. Marcus announced that was the one Darcie was at. I turned up the volume.

"A joint task force consisting of the FBI, local police, and Holst Security stormed the club behind me last night and arrested club owner Scott Flowers. Earlier, FBI Agent Kent Moore explained to me that Mr. Flowers was a known drug dealer, and thanks to a slip-up on his part, local police were alerted to his new activity, and they were able to create a quick task force to take the man down. Unfortunately, a Holst Security employee was injured and is at the hospital."

"Darcie." I turned the TV off. "They have to be talking about Darcie."

"You sure about that?"

"Why else would she react the way she did? You would have blown her cover."

He shook his head. "Killian, she's moved on."

"I have to find out if she's okay." I ignored him, refusing to believe she moved on. "Which hospital would they send her to?"

"Killian."

"Doesn't matter. I'll visit all of them."

"Killian!" Marcus snapped, gripping my shoulders. "No hospital will tell you she's in their care. She'll also have protection so no one can get close. Also, what makes you think she'll want to see you?"

Valid points, but I have to try. "I'll call her first."

"You are impossible. I'll give you one more week to get your shit together. The company needs you."

Marcus left, and I immediately dialled Darcie. "You picked up."

"Who is this?" A male voice responded.

Is this her new boyfriend? "Did I dial the right number? I'm trying to reach Darcie Manners."

"You have the right number, but she can't answer the phone right now."

Fear for her knotted my stomach. "Is she okay?"

The male paused. "She'll survive. Who is this?"

"Killian. Killian Pinot."

"Ah, the man who broke my partner's heart." I could hear movement before he spoke again. "You heard the news?"

"Darcie told me not to contact her again, but I was worried." *Tell me she's okay.*

"She received a double dose of a potent rape drug. I almost didn't get to her in time."

Anger boiled. "Did that bastard Scott Flowers touch her?"

"Touch, yes. Rape, no. I rushed her to the hospital for the doctors to cleanse her of the drug. She's asleep and on an IV drip right now. Doctors want to watch her today, but she should be discharged by the end of the day tomorrow."

"What can I do?"

"Let her heal from this first. I will delete this call. Darcie doesn't need to know we talked."

"Wait!" I wanted him to know. I needed someone close to Darcie to know. "I want to apologize."

"Nothing is stopping you."

The man hung up. I stared at my phone. *Nothing is stopping me?* Darcie is stopping me. She ignores my attempts to reach out. If I were to go to her place, she'd leave me at the front door and probably call the cops on me. Call the cops. *That's it!* I'll turn myself in. I can apologize by going to jail, just like she wants. I got ready to go to work. I needed to make sure nothing led to Rarity Inc. or Marcus. It'll take a few days, but it's my only chance.

I asked the front desk officer whom I should talk to about a robbery, and he directed me to the correct department. There I announced who I was and what I'd done. I was handcuffed, informed of my rights, and led to an interview room. My hands were then handcuffed to a table, and then they left me alone.

That is, until someone new came into the room. He introduced himself as FBI Agent Kent Moore — the man involved with the Scott Flowers bust that harmed Darcie. I instantly didn't like him. He began asking me questions, pulling out photos of past heists and wanting to know why I stole those pieces.

I told him everything he wanted to hear. Before he left, I permitted him to go through Rarity Inc. and my house. But, of course, he won't find anything except the mask. Another officer took me out of the interrogation room to a holding cell. I rubbed my wrists where the cuffs had chaffed when they were finally removed and sat on a bench. Closing my eyes and leaning my head back, I can only hope that Marcus won't kill me when the cops arrive at the company. *Did I do the right thing?*

"Why?"

I opened my eyes to see Darcie on the other side of the cell. "For you."

"Me?"

"I wanted to apologize for not telling you who I am. I wanted to explain why I stole and prove that I'm not a bad guy. I wanted to win you back."

"Killian, there is no going back." A sadness filled her hazel eyes. "After everything you told Agent Moore, you will go to jail. Your company will lose its clients and its respect. You'll have nothing."

"I'll have my memories of you, Kitten."

Her breath caught at the nickname. "I don't understand you."

A small smile formed at my next words. "Like a thief, you stole my heart."

She stared at me. I wish I knew what was going through her mind. Then, Darcie's face went blank, and her hands formed fists at her side. I'm unsure if I feel relieved that I told Darcie how I felt or disappointed that she didn't respond. I've exposed myself to her and made myself vulnerable to her. *I really am a mess.*

Agent Moore stepped up behind her, placing a hand on her shoulder. I hated seeing another man touch her. Darcie shrugged off his touch and walked away. My gaze followed her to the door leading out of the cells. She didn't leave. She just stood there.

Agent Moore leaned forward, his voice lowered. "I look forward to putting you in jail."

"Have I ever stolen from you?" I wondered at his dislike of me.

"Not exactly." He answered cryptically.

His gaze shifted toward Darcie. *Does he have a thing for her?* Anger rose in me. I don't want him to go after Darcie now that I'm out of the picture. I did this to bring Darcie closer to me, not to let some other man swoop in. He won't be able to make a case stick. All he has is my confession and the mask.

Two days later, Agent Moore came to me. He informed me that with my confession, the mask he found in my house, and the connection I have to too many of the stolen jewels through

Rarity Inc. I was officially charged with robbery. Numbly I went through the process of moving from the holding cell to an actual jail cell as I awaited trial.

It didn't take long for Marcus to visit. He sat on the other side of the plexiglass, gripping the phone tightly. I kept the connected phone to my ear. As expected, he was pissed. I let him rant. I deserve his anger.

"You done?" I asked calmly.

"Yes. I'm done with you."

"Marcus, I'm sorry I didn't warn you. But, unfortunately, there wasn't enough time. I also knew you'd be mad at me and try to talk me out of this."

"Mad?" His voice went up an octave. "That word doesn't quite cover how I'm feeling."

"The company is clear, and I'm certain nothing is linked to you."

"The company is not clear. It is linked to you. What were you thinking, Killian?"

"Honestly?" I asked cautiously. He nodded. "I did it to try and apologize to Darcie."

He put the phone down and pinched the bridge of his nose. Then, after a moment, he returned the phone to his ear. "I should have known it would come back to her."

"She stole my heart." I said the words quietly.

"I'm sorry, repeat that."

"She stole my heart."

Marcus stared at me, face softening. "You loved Thea."

"I was infatuated with Thea." I corrected.

"You wanted to marry her."

"I was young and stupid. What I feel for Darcie is different."

"You've only known her for a short time."

"I don't know how to explain it. I want her by my side. When she's not, I feel empty. She's an addiction, a drug I don't want to quit. The high she gives me is better than any heist. I'm even considering giving up Le Corbeau for her. I will do anything for Darcie."

"Well fuck." Marcus ran a hand through his hair. "You're serious about her."

"I am."

"Okay. I'm getting you a lawyer."

Chapter Seventeen

Darcie

"It's official." Agent Moore announced proudly. "Killian Pinot has been charged for robbery as Le Corbeau and is awaiting trial."

Why don't I feel happy? "That's excellent news."

"I want you to testify against him."

"Me?"

"He did steal The Eye from around your neck."

"True." I answered slowly, remembering that night. "When is the trial set for?"

"No date yet, but I'll keep you posted." He placed a hand lightly on my arm. "You did an amazing job, Darcie."

Tristan frowned but didn't say anything. Agent Moore pushed the trial with the judge, and within a few short weeks, I was testifying against Killian. I couldn't bring myself to look at him. *This feels wrong.* I know legally this is right. He's a thief, and thieves are criminals, but my gut tells me this is wrong.

I've heard of the lawyer Killian has defending him. He's a shark. So, it surprised me when he never mentioned my brief relationship with him. Instead, he pointed out his non-violent ways and the thieves he was getting ahead of. Agent Moore countered that stealing for whatever reason is against the law. Unfortunately, because nothing was reported as stolen, except for maybe the first two pieces he's ever taken, but even those reports were dropped, there wasn't much of a case, and my testimony covered The Eye only.

The jury deliberated and came back with a not-guilty plea. There wasn't enough physical evidence to convince them he was Le Corbeau. Killian looked back at me, our eyes locked, and I felt something twist my heart. Disappointment? Relief? Lust? Hurt? I couldn't figure out how I felt about the jury's decision. After the verdict to let him go free, I left the courtroom. I went home and looked up the names he mentioned during the trial — Black Fox and Browns Twins.

Down the rabbit hole I went.

Black Fox steals jewels, marble busts, paintings, and anything with a dollar sign. He leaves a little black fox figure behind. Unfortunately, he also leaves behind bodies if anyone gets in his way — whether it is on his way in or out. The Browns Twins have a record for their thefts and dealings on the dark web. They are in it for the money. From what I could find, they would even destroy their thefts to sell them to multiple buyers.

Suddenly Le Corbeau's heists seem humane compared to them. All this research has me even more confused about Killian. He's still a thief but is protecting the jewels he's stealing and returning them to the owner — eventually. *He's like a Robin Hood for jewels.* If I forget that Killian is Le Corbeau — a criminal, a fact that I just can't seem to let go of — then maybe there could have been something between us. Not only is he good-looking, but he is also intelligent, funny, has a good heart, and is charming.

Chapter Eighteen

♥

Le Corbeau

After the not guilty verdict, Marcus collected me from jail. He didn't utter a word as he drove me home. He just dropped me off and left. My home was a mess. Agent Moore went through every nook and cranny trying to find evidence against me. Not that he would have found anything.

I remembered the looks he kept giving Darcie throughout the trial. At first, I thought it was because he feared our relationship would be brought up, ruining her credibility. I ensured the lawyer Marcus got me knew nothing of our time in Paris. He seemed desperate to have me kept behind bars. *He must have fallen for her charm as I did.* Agent Moore's actions, and the looks he gave Darcie, were of a man lusting after a woman. Now that I'm found innocent in the eyes of the law, I wonder what Darcie and Agent Moore will do.

Darcie has always said she wanted to see me in handcuffs and have me arrested. Unless I was seeing what I wanted to see, it looked like she was relieved the verdict came to a not guilty plea. It took everything I had to resist the urge to call her. But, after hearing the truth behind my heists during the trial, it might be best to let her process. *I'll go see her tomorrow.*

In the meantime, I cleaned. It had gotten late, and the heavy rain outside reflected how I felt internally. About to head upstairs for the night, the doorbell rang. *Whom could that be?* I stared at the door. It's not Marcus. He would have just waltzed right in like he always does. The doorbell rang again. Irritated at the late hour, I swung the door open ready to snap at the person on the other side, only to stare dumbfounded at the soaked beauty before me.

"Darcie?" *I must be hallucinating.*

"Can I come in?" She questioned through chattering teeth.

I shook my head, clearing it and stepped aside. "What are you doing here?"

"I don't know."

"How did you know where I live?"

She barely managed a smile. "I have my sources."

Locking the door, I rushed upstairs to grab her a towel. "You're soaked."

She let me towel dry her hair so it no longer dripped onto the entryway floor. Then, she finally spoke as I moved the towel down her arms.

"Killian, do you steal so that others don't feel the same loss your mother did when the family ring was stolen and never returned?"

I stopped to stare at her. *Of course, she came with questions.* She took the towel from me, removing some of the water that had soaked her.

"Partly. I started breaking into homes when I was young, looking for my mother's ring. Then I met Thea, the woman who threw herself on me back in Paris."

She paused at her legs to scowl at me. "Your ex."

I smiled, enjoying the bitter tone from her. "Yes. Together we started stealing — for fun. I fell for her, wanted to marry her. Then she nearly had me sent to prison."

"How?"

"She purposely set off alarms to aid in her escape. I barely got out. This was around the time when I started Rarity Inc. If it wasn't for Marcus and my company, I wouldn't be where I am right now."

We had migrated from the entryway to the living room. I picked up the tossed cushions and placed them back on the couch. Darcie wrapped the towel around her shoulders, cocooning herself with it like a shield before taking a seat. I sat next to her, keeping a respectable distance between us.

"How could you go back to stealing after such a betrayal?"

"Marcus' love for the history of the pieces we appraise reminded me why I got into this business. And his passionate hatred toward the thieves who have stolen precious pieces from innocent people."

We sat on the couch in silence. I itched to touch her, to kiss her, to have her look at me. But, instead, Darcie's grip on the towel tightened, and she appeared to be deep in thought. Did the truth behind my actions help her see I'm not quite the criminal she's been determined to paint me as? I watched her, afraid she'd scurry away if I made a sound.

"My ex hurt me." She started. "He won me over quickly with his charm and made me feel important, beautiful, and loved. After some time, that charm washed away to show his darker colours. It took me a while to figure out that was his real personality and not just stress from work. Around the same time, I discovered he was charming someone new. He lied to me, hurt me, and taught me to be cautious around men. Then I met you." Darcie looked at me, and guilt hit me hard. "You charmed me, charmed my friends, then revealed that you were lying. That hurt Killian."

"I'm sorry." I whispered, knowing those words would sound meaningless to her after that tale. "I was going to tell you the truth. Eventually."

"Even after learning that you're Le Corbeau, I couldn't get you out of my head." She continued like I never spoke. "I thought burying myself in work would help, but it didn't. I thought I'd be happy seeing a thief like you behind bars, but instead, I felt pained seeing you there and, even worse seeing you on trial."

"Darcie."

"Killian, you've ruined me. Broke through my barriers so effortlessly and stole from me."

I knitted my brows together, not sure what she meant. I held my breath, hoping for the words I had dreamed about.

"You stole my heart."

With that, she leaned forward and kissed me. Tentative. As if she was afraid that she may have been too late. I instantly reacted. Lacing a hand behind her head, I deepened the kiss. I put everything into that kiss.

"Let's get you out of those wet clothes before you catch a cold." I murmured against her lips.

"A hot shower would be nice."

An image of water running down her body filled my mind. "Of course."

Taking her hand, I led her upstairs to the bathroom. Once inside, lips and hands collided as clothes were hastily removed. We stood under the hot spray, kissing and caressing. I licked the water from her skin, sending shivers through her frame. Soft moans escaped her lips when my mouth formed around her breast. Fingers buried deep inside, pumping and rubbing along her clit until she was about to climax. Then I got down on my knees to finish her off with my mouth. My name on Darcie's lips is the sweetest sound I've ever heard.

"Got the chill off?" I teased, standing to turn off the water.

A blush graced her cheeks. *I'll never tire of seeing that.*

"You are a devil with that tongue."

"I will take that as a compliment." Then, with a grin, I handed her a fresh towel. "Now that you're clean, what do you say about getting dirty?"

"What exactly are you getting at?"

"There's a bed just beyond this door."

"Your point?" There was a playfulness in her tone.

Sweeping her in my arms, I carried her to the bedroom, dumping her onto the bed. "My point is that we should make good use of it."

She laughed as I rolled on a condom and joined her on the bed. *She is mine.* Holding her wrists on either side of her head, I trailed my lips along her body. I was learning where she was most sensitive and pulling various sounds from her. She squirmed under me. She whimpered when I avoided her breasts and trailed lower down her body. *Patience.* The more I teased her, the stronger her need for me became.

"Killian." Darcie let out a whimper. "Please."

"Please, what?" I kissed her inner thigh.

"I need you."

150

Music to my ears. "And I, you, Darcie."

"Then take me already. I can't take much more."

"Are you sure you're ready for me?" I teased.

I was coming back up her body. I hovered over her. Lining myself up, I was ready to plunge into her depths.

"Yes." She lifted her hips, urging me.

Lips on hers, I buried myself deep. She cried into my mouth. *Fuck she's tight.* I let her adjust to my size. When Darcie shifted, I took that as my queue to move. Slow at first but with her arms around me urging me faster, harder, I complied with her every wish. Her nails scraped at my back when her release came, and her walls tightened pleasurably around me. Just a few more strokes and my release followed.

I kissed her deeply before rolling to the side, pulling her with me. Laying on my back with Darcie atop me, I ran fingers gently along her spine. *This is pure bliss.* This is a moment I never want to end. While in the after-sex silence, I couldn't help but think of two things. One: I love her. Two: I want to marry her. That second thought made me pause. *Am I ready to consider marriage?* The concept didn't work well with Thea, but I can picture a future with Darcie.

"What are you thinking?" Darcie propped her chin onto my chest.

"Just picturing what I'm going to do to you next?"

"Care to show and tell?" She smiled.

With a smile of my own, I rolled her back under me. "My pleasure."

Changing condoms, I flipped Darcie onto her stomach, ordering her to hold onto the headboard. On her knees with her ass in the air, I wrapped an arm around her waist, fingers playing with her folds. I kissed a trail along her spine. I prepped her for entry. Gripping her hips, I slammed into her in one hard stroke.

"Killian!" She cried out with a moan.

I didn't hold back this time. Instead, I moved hard and fast. The feel of her tight around me was invigorating. The sound of flesh slapping against flesh mixed with moans and pants filled the room. She was close to her release. I could feel it. Slowing my pace, Darcie whimpered a complaint which turned to a gasp as my hand came around to play with her clit. I took a few teasing strokes before I picked up speed, then slowed again.

"Darcie." I whispered her name, kissing the back of her neck. "You've stolen my heart."

Epilogue

Darcie

A single streak of sunlight fell across my face waking me up. I kicked off the sheets and stretched my arms over my head before going to the bathroom to relieve my bladder. After a quick shower and fresh clothes, I went to the kitchen. *Are those pancakes I smell?* Killian stood in my kitchen cooking.

"What are you doing here?"

He turned a brilliant smile on me. "Morning, beautiful."

He plated two pancakes, drenched them in real maple syrup, and then slid it onto the breakfast bar for me. "Killian, what are you doing here?"

"I thought we could spend it together since you have a day off."

How thoughtful. My heart swelled. "I already have plans with Tristan."

"Cancel them." His kiss made me want to. "I'll make it worthwhile."

I think I might have whined as he pulled away. "I can't."

"What has got you so busy these past few weeks?" He started washing the dishes.

I smiled. "A personal project."

He glanced upwards as if trying to peer through the ceiling to my office space. "Can I see?"

"You won't find anything upstairs."

His phone chimed. "Looks like I don't have today free anyway."

"Marcus keeping you busy?" I questioned, sinking my teeth into a perfectly fluffy pancake. *Thank you, Marcus.*

"Seems that way." Killian gave me one long deep kiss. "See you tonight?"

"Maybe." I teased.

"I hope so. I miss you, Darcie."

I urged him out of my place. I finished eating, then grabbed my phone and keys before heading to Tristan's apartment. He answered the door shirtless, a fact he liked to tease me about when I ordered him to cover up. Fully dressed, he poured coffee into a travel mug, then we were out the door.

Without Killian's knowledge, I began researching the theft of his mother's ring. Tristan was helping me with the research, and Marcus, once I was getting somewhere, was helping to keep Killian away so I could secretly find the ring. It took some begging and a promise on my part to have Agent Moore get me the police file. The file on the theft was skinny, almost useless, so Tristan and I had worked hard on tracking down the lead detective. Today we are visiting him.

An elderly man in his late forties or early fifties answered the door. "Whatever you're selling, I'm not buying."

"We're not selling anything." I assured him. "My name is Darcie, and this is Tristan. Are you Martin?"

"What if I am?"

"We were wondering if we could ask you a few questions about an old case of yours."

Martin eyed us suspiciously. "What case?"

"It's about a ring theft from a woman named Mrs. Pinot."

"Come in." He ushered us inside, scanning the area outside before closing the door. "Who sent you?"

"No one sent us." Tristan assured him. "We came because you were the lead detective on the case, and we wanted to know if there was anything you might remember that wasn't put into the case file."

"Sit down." Martin closed the front curtains. "Why are you two young things interested in this old case?"

I glanced at Tristan. *What has him so paranoid?* "I'm dating Mrs. Pinot's son, and I was hoping I might be able to find the ring for him. He's been searching for it for years."

"He won't find it."

"Why not?"

"Because, young lady, there's a conspiracy."

"Excuse me?"

"Wait here." Martin shuffled out of the room.

"Maybe we should have checked his medical records." Tristan whispered. "Something is loose in his head."

"I heard that." Martin called back to us as he returned with a box.

I jumped up to take it from him. "What's all this?"

"My research into that ring." Placing it on the coffee table, he sat and began pulling out papers. "This is Mrs. Pinot and her son. She's wearing the ring."

He showed us a picture of the two. *Killian was super cute as a kid.*

"I searched that house from top to bottom. There was no sign of a break-in, and the only fingerprints I could find were of the two Pinots."

"Was there no husband in the picture?"

He shook his head. "Deadbeat dad left them when the kid was two. I looked into him, but he wasn't in the same province. So my captain at the time insisted I drop the case."

"Why would he do that?" Tristan questioned. "Clearly, a ring did exist."

Martin's eyes sparkled. "That's what I thought, so in my free time, I kept searching."

"What did you find?" Excitement coursed through me with the hope of actually finding the ring.

"A conspiracy." At our questioning faces, he explained. "I found other women who have claimed thefts of their jewellery over a five-year span, and their cases were also dropped. The link: my captain. I was fired before I got too close to the truth."

"What connection did your captain have to these cases? Besides being the one to want them closed and forgotten."

Martin shifted through the papers he had pulled out. "Mrs. Pinot told me she had a blind date with someone she met online the night prior to her noticing the ring was gone. Unfortunately, she couldn't remember anything about the man she was with, so I looked into it." He pulled out a sketch artist's rendition of a bearded male. "The staff from the restaurant they went to remembered the couple, and this sketch was made of the man. That is my captain."

He pulled out a picture of his captain for reference. Tristan held the two pieces side by side. "The resemblance is unmistakable. What did your captain say when you brought this to his attention?"

"He fired me."

"On what grounds?"

"Unlawful use of police resources."

"That's not right!" I gaped at him.

"Times were different back then." He shrugged. "But I didn't stop. I discovered he was the mystery date of every woman whose jewellery was stolen."

"Why didn't they speak up if they remembered him?"

"That's just it. They didn't remember him. At least not right away. I spoke to these women months, even years, after their jewellery was stolen. The image of the man came to them over time, but when I showed them the picture, they remembered him clearly."

"What about Mrs. Pinot?"

"She was too distraught over losing her ring that she couldn't remember the captain, even with the picture."

"Looks like we need to track down your captain and have a chat with him." Tristan claimed.

"Good luck." Martin chuckled. "Every time I go see him trying to get a confession out of him in his old age, he pretends to have amnesia — or maybe it is dementia. I can never remember the difference between the two."

"You know where he is?"

"Embassy Senior Living. Ask the receptionist for Carl and Amy South."

"Thank you, Martin." I still held the picture of Killian and his mom. "Do you mind if I take this?"

He smiled, shaking his head. "If you two manage to get the stolen jewellery back, or even a recorded confession, make sure you come back. This case ruined my career as a police officer, and it's been haunting me since."

"Of course."

Tristan and I left him. I continued to stare at the picture. Killian's mom was a beautiful woman. It's too bad I haven't been able to meet her. Seeing this ring again, I'm sure, would bring a smile to both her face and Killian's.

The receptionist at the senior home greeted us with a bright smile. Tristan beamed at her and turned on the charm. He explained whom we were looking for and requested to see Carl's medical file. She seemed hesitant. I explained that we were here about an old case of his when he was in uniform, and we wanted to make sure we would not upset him with our questions. Finally, with the health of their residents on the line, she reluctantly agreed. She went through the door behind her and returned to show us the file. No amnesia or dementia for him, but the wife has a weak heart. *Note to self: separate the two before questioning Carl.*

We went to Captain Carl's room with visitor passes clipped to our shirts. A nurse answered the door. She seemed thrilled that someone was coming to visit the South couple. Then, with a gentle warning to not over-excite Amy, she left us alone with the elderly couple.

"Who are you?" Carl snarled suspiciously.

"Friends of Martin's." I stated. "Nice room."

"Martin?" He chuckled. "That old fool doesn't have any friends."

"He's a good cop."

"Would you two like anything to drink?" Amy questioned sweetly. "I can have a nurse fetch you a drink."

"Thank you, Amy, but we're fine." Tristan smiled at her.

"I should leave if you have business to discuss with my husband. I'm not allowed to listen in when he discusses business."

I sat beside her on the couch, gently taking her hand. "What a lovely ring."

"You like it? Carl bought it for our anniversary." She turned to him. "Where did you get it again, dear?"

"The place is closed."

She seemed distraught by that. "That's too bad."

"Amy." I pulled her attention back to me. "I hear there's a very nice garden here. Do you want to go for a walk?"

"Walk?" A giggle bubbled up in her. "Dear, you'll have to push me around in a wheelchair. I can't walk very far."

"I'm okay with that." I helped her off the couch and over to the wheelchair. "We won't be long. I'll let you two talk."

Tristan smiled at me as I took Amy out of the room. No need to have her hear all the truthful accusations we have against her husband and his thieving ways. *How am I going to get this ring back?* I pushed Amy around in the garden leisurely. Stopping when she asked me to so she could smell flowers.

"My husband did something bad, didn't he?" She asked me suddenly.

"What makes you say that?"

"I know he didn't buy this ring. He couldn't, not on his salary."

I stopped at a bench, locked her wheelchair and sat down. "No, he didn't buy that ring."

Tears welled up in her eyes. "You know how he got it don't you?"

"I do."

"Tell me."

With a deep breath, I took her hand. "He loves you very much."

"I would have been happy with a plastic ring from a cereal box."

I couldn't tell her about all the thefts her husband did. "He stole this ring."

Tears flowed from her eyes. "Stole it? As in from evidence?"

I bit my lower lip and whispered. "No."

"From someone?" She wiped at her tears and pulled the ring off. "Be a dear and return it to its owner. If I had known, I would have made Carl do that years ago."

I folded the ring in my palm. *I'm sorry.* I sat there with Amy as she struggled to gather her strength. Before returning her to Carl, I took her to the bathroom to gently wash her face, removing the evidence of tears. However, I could do nothing about her reddened eyes. A quick text to Tristan telling him we were just outside the door would give him enough warning to end his conversation with Carl.

Amy immediately railed her husband for being an idiot. Tristan and I left them. I showed him the ring telling him that Amy knew Carl didn't buy it but didn't know it was stolen and wanted it returned. We returned to Martin to inform him of our trip to the senior home. He was so thankful and relieved that at least one piece of jewellery was being returned. He even invited us over again for coffee and conversation.

Tristan returned us to his apartment. "You going to give that to Killian now?"

"It belongs to his family."

He grinned. "It's been what? A year since the trial?"

"About there. Why?" The statement seemed so out of place.

"He really makes you happy?"

I couldn't help but smile. "He really does."

"And you're okay with him stealing?"

"Not at all." I sighed. "But I'm okay with him protecting treasures from worse people."

Tristan chuckled. "You want lunch?"

"Yes, please."

"So." He started as he pulled out the ingredients for grilled cheese. "Have you told him about Agent Moore?"

I grimaced. "Not yet."

"You should. You're leaving next week."

"I know."

The promise I made with Agent Moore for the case file was that I'd work with him at the FBI for two cases. I haven't figured out how to tell Killian yet. Tristan and I sat on the couch, eating and watching a movie. Afterwards, I texted Killian telling him I'll be over tonight. Then I stopped off at a craft store for a ring box. I went to Killian's early and found him taking food out of takeout boxes in the kitchen.

"Cheater." I teased.

He grinned. "How was your day?"

"Eventful."

"What did you and Tristan do?"

I smiled. "We visited a retired cop and chatted about a past case."

He frowned. "Did you see that detective? What was her name, Kyrie Albert?"

"No. But I did reach out to her the other day, and we chatted over the phone."

"So, she remembers you?"

"As if we hadn't stopped talking. She's excited for the next chapter in my life."

"Next chapter?" He took the plates of food over to the dining table.

Now or never. "I'm going to be leaving next week."

"For work?"

"Sort of." I wasn't sure how he was going to take the news. "I'm going to work with Agent Moore."

A shadow crossed his features. "The FBI agent? The one who tried to put me in jail? For how long?"

"Firstly, he only did that because I brought Le Corbeau to his attention and wanted the thief arrested. Secondly, I don't know. It's a trial run to see if I want to shift careers and become an FBI agent."

"Is this why I haven't seen much of you?" He accused.

"No! Agent Moore has been trying to get me to join the FBI since before Paris. However, I only recently agreed to work two cases for him on a trial period only."

"But you could end up loving it and staying with him."

I frowned at him. "I love working at Holst Security."

"Then why are you doing this?"

I chewed my bottom lip. "This is the promise I made for the information he could provide."

"What information could he have provided that you couldn't get on your own?" He held up a hand, not wanting to hear an answer from me. "It would have been nice if you told me sooner. We could have discussed this instead of you dropping this information in my lap." Killian ran a hand through his hair. "I don't like Agent Moore. I don't like how he looks at you. I don't like the thought of you working so closely with him."

I fell silent, biting my tongue from what I wanted to say. *Then put a ring on it.* Agent Moore never interested me like Killian seems to think he's interested in me. We ate for a bit before he told me about the new location of Rarity Inc. that he and Marcus have been working on. He spoke so that we weren't in silence. If I didn't bring up Agent Moore, he would have been more excited to tell me his news. I helped him clean the table before going to grab the ring from my coat.

"Maybe this will make up for my sudden leaving announcement. But, just so you know, this is why I needed Agent Moore's information."

He looked down at the ring box I placed on the counter. His lips quirked as if he was fighting to stay mad at me. He couldn't hold back as his lips tilted into a playful smirk. "Darcie Manners, are you proposing to me?"

"Just open the box."

Curious, he lifted the lid and stared. "Is this?"

I pulled the picture Martin let me have out of my back pocket. "Your mother's ring? Yes, it is."

He took the picture staring at it and then at the ring. "How did you find it?"

"I talked to a retired cop today." I reminded him. "He never stopped looking. He's the one who found out who stole the ring. He was just never able to find the ring itself — or get a confession."

Killian put the ring down and swept me up in his arms for a kiss. "Marry me."

I laughed. "I knew you'd like it."

He pulled a ring box out of a junk drawer opening it to reveal a beautiful diamond ring. Instead of taking that one, he grabbed his mother's ring and bent on one knee. "Darcie Manners, will you marry me?"

"You're serious?"

"You make me happy, Darcie. With this ring, I want the world to know that no one else but me can make you happy. Please be forever mine."

My heart swelled at his confession. Unable to form words, I only nodded and slipped my finger into the ring. Killian stood, crashing his lips onto mine. Wrapping his arms around me, he held me close.

"I love you Darcie."

"And I you, Killian." My eyes drifted down to the diamond he had left on the counter. "I hope you can get your money back."

"You are going to wear the diamond while working with Agent Moore. I want him to see that you're taken, and quite honestly, I don't want this ring to go missing while you're working. I'll wed you with my mother's ring when you return."

Glossary

Le Corbeau ~ The Crow
   Bonjour ~ Good morning
   Veronica à été arretée ~ Veronica was arrested
   Meutre ~ Murder
   Je suis desolée ~ I am sorry
   Vous avez essayé de m'appeler ~ You tried to call me
   Je sais ~ I know
   Oui ~ Yes
   C'est aussi mon amie ~ She is my friend too
   Es-tu prêt pour le déjeuner ~ Are you ready for lunch
   Je ne peux pas ~ I can't
   J'ai une réunion d'affaires ~ I'm having a business meeting
   Enchanté ~ Nice to meet you
   Vous pouvez vous joindre à nous ~ You can join us
   Je suppose que oui ~ I guess so
   Mais, elle a pleuré toute la nuit ~ But, she cried all night
   Ce n'est pas ta faute ~ It is not your fault
   Mon amie ~ My friend
   Oui, bien sûr ~ Why, yes, of course

Si vous êtes réel ~ If you are real

Qu'est-ce que c'est ~ What is that

Venez ~ Come

Mr. Lux et Mr. Pinot de Rarity Inc. sont ici ~ Mr. Lux and Mr. Pinot from Rarity Inc. are here

Merci Gerald ~ Thank you Gerald

Envoyez-les à la chambre forte ~ Please send them to the vault

Bien sûr ~ Of course

Je comprends ~ I understand

C'est important ~ Is it important

Quoi ~ What

Ici ~ Here

Non ~ No

Qu'avez-vous trouvé ~ What did you find

C'est tout ~ Is that all

Vous avez terminé ~ Are you finished here

Il y a quelque chose ici ~ There is something here

Trop tard ~ Too late

Mesdames ~ Ladies

Ma belle ~ My beautiful

Vous m'avez volé ~ You stole from me

Je ne l'ai pas fait ~ I did not

Je ne sais pas de quoi vous parlez ~ I don't know what you're talking about

Tu vas bien ~ Are you alright

Elle m'a sauvé ~ She saved me

Merci ~ Thank you

About Author

Ivy Marie grew up an army brat. Moving every two or three years, and finally settling in Ottawa, Ontario, Canada. When she's not writing she's at work, or spending time with her friends.

Both friends and family are supportive of her creative expression. She's found comfort in Supernatural Romance, with werewolves and vampires as the main creatures she writes about, and also in Contemporary Romance.

Ivy Marie writes for her own enjoyment. She also hopes that the joy she feels while writing is expressed and passed on to you.

Connect

♥

I really appreciate you reading my book! Here are my social media coordinates;

Facebook: www.facebook.com/IvysStolenHearts
Instagram: ivymariebooks
Blue Sky: @ivymarie-author.bsky.social
X: @IvyMarie_Books
Website: www.ivymarieauthor.com

Don't forget about my wonderful cover artist - Shawna Russ;

Instagram: shawncolourart

Also By

Keep an eye out other books by Ivy Marie.

Contemporary Romance
Thief in Paris
Bad Decisions (Book 1 of Decisions Duet)
Late Decisions (Book 2 of Decisions Duet)
Surprised by Love ~ Coming 2025
Fan the Flames ~ Coming 2026

Paranormal Romance
Stolen Heart
His Hunter
Bound to the Reaper (Book 1 of Reaper)
Reaper Undercover (Book 2 of Reaper) ~ Coming 2026
Reaper Forever (Book 3 of Reaper) ~ Coming 2027
Witch Troubles ~ Coming 2025

Like Hell series (Paranormal Romance) ~ Coming 2028

IVY MARIE

Like Hell Mario (Prequel)
Like Hell this is Real (Book 1)
Like Hell this is Normal (Book 2)
Like Hell this is Happening (Book 3)
Like Hell Alternative (Alternate Reality)